NEFARIUM

AN INAMORATA NOVEL

NAKIA COOK

VEILED THREATS PUBLICATIONS

NEFARIUM

AN INAMORATA NOVEL

Nefarium: An Inamorata Novel

First edition October 2024

Veiled Threats Publications

ISBN 978-1-0689918-0-6 (e-book)

ISBN 978-1-7381315-9-4 (paperback)

ALSO BY THE AUTHOR

Inamorata: A Rosewood Hollow Novel

Salarius: An Inamorata Novella, Book 2

Drummer Boy: A Short Story

The Deed: A Left Hand Duology Prequel Novella (paperback)

The Haunting of Jamal Jackson: The Left Hand Duology, Book 1

Nefarium

An abomination; breaking natural laws.

CHAPTER ONE

Rukhsana set the table for breakfast, hoping her father would hurry and join her before she left for work. They spent little time together, and today was a great opportunity to rectify the situation. The silverware clinked the plate as she laid them on the table. Pleased, she stepped back to admire the spread. She'd forgotten something.

Inside the cluttered pantry, she searched the shelf for her father's favorite breakfast condiment. Second favorite. This was the first year she'd attempted to make a batch of strawberry preserves on her own. They hadn't come out half bad, according to Abi. "Just like your mama used to make," he said, smiling with his eyes. She returned his smile, not believing him. When it came to her mother's recipes, she lost confidence in her abilities.

Rukhsana palmed the jar and headed towards the stove. "Shoot!"

Acrid black smoke wafted from the cast-iron skillet as grease splattered the stovetop and the floor. She switched off the burning beef sausages. The curtains billowed in the opened window, pushing the smoke into her face. Regrettably, she had just loosened the twists in her hair, and now she was going to stink like smoke for the rest of the day.

Along with the burnt sausages, the stench of sulfur wafted into the room, stopping her dead in her tracks. She waited a moment in case her nose was playing tricks. Prickly sensations traveled down her spine as movement on the opposite side of the kitchen confirmed her suspicions. The thing she'd hoped to avoid was happening again.

Scratching noises directed her attention to the stainless steel refrigerator door. Rukhsana waved the greasy black smoke away from her face. She glanced at the staircase across from the kitchen entrance. Empty. Abu was still upstairs; the poor man was running late, thank God.

Sunbeams streaming in from the skylight retreated. The kitchen dimmed, taking away any semblance of a peaceful morning. The trespasser came to her father's house twice this week already, startling her in the bath for the first time, and in the laundry room yesterday. She had no idea what caused those visitations and now it was here again. But why? What in the world triggered these intrusions? The figure lifted a clawed hand and her heart lurched.

"Rukhsana." Dread washed over her. She hated when they spoke. The gravelly nature of spectral voices rattled her brain. To make matters worse, this one knew her name. The more demons knew about you, the stronger they became. Somewhere in the last few days, she'd made a mistake, attracting this one's attention. Knowing that something she'd done made it want to get to know her was unsettling.

"Rukhsana... Rukhsana!"

Eyes cast down, she crept in the opposite direction, away from the creature's voice. Behind her, she heard a scuffle. The invisible barriers separating the ethereal from the material world fell; its fist pounded against the fridge door.

The demon started for her, crossing the kitchen, its bare feet slapping the tiles. From the corner of her eye, she watched the being slink in her direction. Her heart pounded, a deafening rhythm that reverberated through her entire chest. She backed away, desperately searching her mind for a way to banish the entity.

Normally, her extra morning prayers kept them at bay, but she'd neglected her preventative measures over the last few days. Rather than soothe her, the constant attention to her religious routine left her with a profound sense of burden and mental heaviness. Overcome by deep weariness, she took a break. The trouble with breaks is that the wicked never need them.

"I know you can hear me, Rukhsana. Look at me!" The sound of its voice, which was a little like a young girl's, and a lot like a dying cat, threatened to break her resolve.

Most jinn weren't clever and she hated when they took her by surprise like this, shifting the power dynamic in their favor. She moved about the kitchen in haste, ignoring the figure standing in her peripheral vision. *They thrive on fear. Don't offer ammunition.* If she ignored it or appeared indifferent, maybe she could get out of this without incident.

Although that was the plan, she couldn't help stealing a glance at the creature. Its top half resembled a teen girl while its bottom half moved about on rickety, bowed legs. A low, guttural sound emanated from within the being, causing shudders throughout her body. "Hey, stupid whore. I'm talking to you," it snarled.

So much for ignoring it. Rukhsana sucked her teeth in annoyance. *Fine. If you want to play it that way.* She headed towards the sink. The jinni bumped the table as it scuttled around it. Cut off, it forced her to acknowledge its presence.

Rukhsana planted her feet and launched herself from the hip, aiming her upper body at the creature's midsection. With her hands, she pushed it away from her body. It stumbled into the kitchen island with a thud and fell over the counter in an unnatural arc. Rukhsana winced at the sickening sound of cracking backbones.

She backed away from it and shook out the mild frostnip in her hands. Touching supernatural creatures didn't unsettle Rukhsana as much as it used to. Over time, she'd learned that the icy burns faded after a massage to the affected area once she applied a quarter-sized amount of black seed oil. She made a mental note to buy some from work. There'd been so much activity in the past few days that she'd run out.

The home invasions were a mounting problem. She'd grown up seeing things that weren't there; a man or woman who moved in ways that didn't seem right, a dog that didn't quite look like a dog, scampering into an alley. But never at home. They wouldn't dare cross the threshold and step foot into her father's house. Not with Mama around.

Now that her mother was gone, Rukhsana saw them all the time, and while that was an issue, the real problem was getting them to leave.

Each one fought harder than the last. She relied on different tactics to expel them and feared she was running out of ideas.

"Look at you, putting up a fight, Rukhsana. It's like you think you're invincible." The jinni girl bared jagged teeth at her as it inched closer. It reached out, conjuring whatever metaphysical energy it could before grabbing the jar of strawberry preserves off the counter. It flicked its wrist, launching it at Rukhsana's head. Without hesitation, she ducked. The jar smashed against the wall behind her, coating the bottom of her pant legs with red slivers of glass and chunks of strawberries from her late mother's garden.

Rukhsana sighed. *Enough of this.* She narrowed her eyes, staring into the icy blue ones on the wicked girl's face. She reached for the antique plant mister she kept on the windowsill above the sink. The girl's blood-red lips cracked open and her oversized forked tongue slithered out, making lewd gestures towards Rukhsana.

"Don't you want to join your mother in hell?" the girl jeered with her distorted voice. She squatted and released the odor of sulfur and excrement into the air. Rukhsana reared back, gagging and choking. She pointed the can towards her and pressed the lever, spraying her with Zamzam water.

The girl's smug expression switched to horror. She let out a blood-curdling scream. Rukhsana sprayed a steady stream of holy water, backing the creature into a corner. Skin on its cheeks and forehead darkened and cracked. The flesh sloughed away, revealing the grayish, blistered dermis underneath. The jinni's eyes glowed white-hot at the outer edges.

It clawed at the remaining bits of bubbling flesh, tossing them to the floor, revealing a bluish-gray layer of muscle underneath. Rukhsana heard it hiss. Her mouth went dry. Its feet stamped and scratched as it threatened to charge. She raised her hand, promising to spray it again, and the creature scurried into a dark corner, out of range of the holy water.

"You alright down there, Roxie?" Rukhsana watched the demon turn towards the staircase. Her father stood at the top, unable to see the cowering beast from that height.

"I'm okay, Abi," Rukhsana said.

"Why don't you come on down here? I could use a hand." The jinni said, mimicking her voice. It licked its cracked lips and smiled.

"If you insist," her father said.

"No!" Rukhsana said, rushing towards the doorway, water bottle in hand. "Don't come down."

"Well, which is it? Should I come down now or not?"

"No, Abi. I need to clean the floor first... I spilled something. I'll call you once I've finished; it's pretty nasty," Rukhsana said, glaring at the creature.

The frequent, inconvenient appearances by the jinn made it increasingly difficult to hide these incidents from her father. He already thought she was crazy enough without having to explain that spectral beings were popping up in the house every day. It troubled her, but the situation was hers to bear alone.

"I'll be honest, sweetheart, it doesn't smell that appetizing down there anyway," her father said as he returned to his bedroom. When his door closed, Rukhsana unscrewed the cap from the mister and rushed the demon, dousing it from head to toe. It erupted into a ball of smokeless fire and careened towards the gas stove.

"Oh, no you don't," Rukhsana said, swinging at it with the broom. The flaming body of the jinni swirled and pivoted on its feet before regrouping and coming at her. It grabbed her with its elongated fingers and pushed her to the floor.

Rukhsana bucked and tossed it off, smothering the flames that licked at her sleeves, then scrambled across the floor, getting ground bits of glass stuck in her palms. The jinni caught her by the back of the head. It locked its fingers in her thick hair, yanking hard enough that she feared getting whiplash. The odor of singed hair lingered in the air.

She crashed to the floor and wrestled with it, bumping the table. Silverware crashed around her, cracking the tile next to her head. Rukhsana reached for a knife and drove it into the jinni's flaming eye. Although the creature appeared intangible, she felt the blade drive deep inside it. It threw back its head and howled as its body rose to the ceiling, engulfing the room in flames.

"You haven't won yet," the creature said, staring down at Rukhsana from its one intact eye. "She's coming to get you and you're going to die."

A ball of fire flew from the jinni's mouth towards her. She covered her head with her arms and ducked. Deep, icy pains shot through her, then faded. She dropped her arms and peered at the ceiling.

The creature was gone, leaving a circle of soot above the kitchen table. She checked her watch and sighed. There were thirty minutes to clean the mess, change, and get to work. Abi would have to fend for himself. At least today, when he ate the greasy breakfast sandwiches he sneaked from the gas station, he'd have good reason.

Rukhsana picked at the glass pieces protruding from her hands and wondered; who was coming to get her?

Chapter Two

"Make sure you keep your hands in the epsom salt. It'll draw out the glass in no time," Iman, the owner of Halal Herbs said. She had one hand in her purse, searching for her car keys while the other one wound a scarf around her neck. The oversized woolen accessory had nothing to do with the weather and everything to do with the youth Quran recital at Salem Islamic Community Center. Iman liked to drink ginger tea with honey and keep her throat warm whenever she taught her students. She spent the day talking in near-whispers, exasperating Rukhsana.

Her customers didn't mind her eccentricities. Perhaps because she had the best prices and most effective natural remedies in town, or maybe they were taken with her striking features. She could tame the most irate customer with her warm smile, high cheekbones and honey-brown skin. Her natural skincare products sold themselves.

"I will, Iman. Thanks for the suggestion," Rukhsana said, submerging her dark brown fists in a bowl of warm, cloudy water. She'd spent her lunch hour hunting for stray pieces of glass in the palms of her hands while replaying the morning's incident in her head.

Iman had been happy to take over her appointments when she visited the doctor's office in the afternoon as the pain became unbearable, but it had been a wasted trip. They hadn't gotten all of the glass out of her hands and they still hurt as much as they had when she'd arrived at work. Her mother would have told her that it was spiritual pain, not physical. Messing around with jinn affected the soul and the body.

She couldn't help but wonder about what the jinni had said. *She* was coming for her. Who was she? And from where was she coming? The list of enemies she'd grown from exorcizing jinn had grown over the years. Jealous people who cursed their would-be lovers through black magic, angry mothers-in-law, any number of people saw her as an adversary. She'd have to be vigilant. Experience told her that anyone could be out for revenge.

"You're welcome, Rukhsana," Iman said, breaking her train of thought. "How many clients do you have this evening? Ah, there they are," Iman palmed her keys.

"None. I'm going to straighten up then lock the—

Rukhsana stopped swishing her hands in the bowl and focused all her attention on the gray-skinned little boy standing next to a display of rosewater remedies. His lips curled into a sneer, making the contents of her stomach flip flop.

"What's wrong?" Iman asked, closing the shop door. "Are you okay? Rukhsana?"

"I-I'm fine," she said, shaking her head. Rukhsana turned away from him to face Iman again. She could see the boy's reflection in the front window.

Iman strode over to her. "You're still seeing them, aren't you?"

"Don't worry about me, Iman, you've got to attend your classes."

"We both know they can start without me. They know it better than I do. Now, honey, listen. You need to talk to your father about these visions you're having."

"You know I can't do that," Rukhsana said.

"Then see an imam at another masjid if you don't want him to know about it. Hear me out," Iman said, throwing up her hands. "It's just a consultation, you're not betraying your father by seeking unbiased counsel."

"I'm fine, Iman. I don't need to see anyone. I'm a raqiyah, I expel demons all the time. I need to figure out why they're showing themselves to me with such frequency," she said, chewing on a nail. "There has to be a logical explanation."

"What's logical about jinn? Honey, they're doing it because you're opening yourself up to them. And you need to hurry up and close yourself off."

"I'm working on it. Anyway, go on, get out of here."

"Should you be alone with... whatever you're seeing? Should I wait for you?"

"Nah," Rukhsana shook her head. "I'm fine."

"Aren't you afraid? It kind of gives me the creeps knowing there's a presence in here." Iman's head swiveled, looking from one end of the store to the next at nothing in particular, unsure of what to fear.

"Nope. They annoy me more than anything. Jinn are a nuisance, but very few are actually dangerous."

"If you say so," Iman said, gesturing to Rukhsana's injured hands. "I've witnessed an exorcism before. Demonic possession and all of that supernatural stuff gives me the willies," Iman said, grabbing Rukhsana's shoulder. "If you change your mind, Imam Yahya said he'd be glad to assist you."

"Thanks, but no thanks. I've got this."

"Where is it? The... whatever it is. Is it near me?" Iman spun in a circle and looked over her shoulder at nothing.

"No. It's behind me. I can see its reflection in the window," Rukhsana said.

"You can see it right now?" Iman asked her.

"Yes. It's right there." She jabbed a thumb over her shoulder. Rukhsana put on a brave face for Iman, but she was screaming inside. Most of the jinni she dealt with were harmless, and while some could inflict physical harm, it was the ones who resembled children that unnerved her.

Iman screwed up her face and looked behind Rukhsana, then at the window. "Girl, I'm as open as anybody here in Salem, but I really think your father should know what's going on with you. I know it's been hard for you and your dad since your mom passed away Rukhsana, but you've got to bounce back. This is creepy. I'm sure it's taking a toll on your mental health."

Rukhsana flinched at the mention of her mother. Her mother had suffered from relentless attacks from malevolent forces for months before a collapsed roof in her law office left her fighting for her life in a coma. A year ago, she succumbed to her injuries. It felt like yesterday to Rukhsana. From that moment forward, her father had forbidden Rukhsana from performing exorcisms. She hadn't made any promises.

"You're right, Iman. I'll bounce back. I will." The mischievous grin on the boy's dark face challenged her vow, but she was determined not to let Iman see her sweat. Work kept her mind off her grief, and the last thing she needed was to look like a flake in front of her boss.

Being single and child-free allowed Rukhsana time to commit to her job in a way that others couldn't. And there was plenty of work. Things had gotten more competitive in the plaza since the sudden surge in witchcraft over the past five years or so. It seemed like everybody in Salem, Virginia was inspired by the rise in modern paganism, and had declared themselves witches. An array of metaphysical shops opened, offering everything from hand-turned candles to palm reading and seances. Iman's shop, Halal Holy Herbs, stuck out like a sore thumb from the other stores, but the customers were steady. She called it her anti-magic shop.

Iman paid Rukhsana to oversee her special-needs customers and provide recommendations for those who struggled with debilitating health issues, like high blood pressure, diabetes and rheumatoid arthritis. Rukhsana's nursing degree was an immense boon to her job.

After regular store hours, Rukhsana opened the backroom for those who had more sinister internal sufferings. This darker aspect of her career had been reluctantly inherited during her upbringing. By her early teens, she had memorized the Quran and started her training in the art of exorcism. Her mother said it was a gift. That she was a natural successor to her parents who made house calls to those who found themselves unable to pray or visit a mosque without incident.

Rukhsana's father encouraged her to recite and pray for the afflicted people, and for years, she resisted. She opted to stay back at the masjid and play with the other little girls. She didn't want to visit weird people and pray. There were better ways to spend her time.

"It's time you start learning the art of protecting yourself from the shaytaan," her mother said.

"But why? My friends don't have to do all this extra stuff. They just pray when it's time and that's it," Rukhsana said.

"The closer you get to Allah, the more the devil will come for you."

"I thought you didn't want me to get involved?"

"I don't," her mother had said. "But your father insists. How about we do it for his sake?"

Unlike her mother, she went on thinking it unfair that her religious duties entailed such a burden. She was a normal girl, seeking a normal life. She even envied the young nuns she saw traveling to and from the tiny parish at the end of their street. They dressed a lot like her, prayed and devoted themselves to God, but exorcisms weren't a part of their duties, (she'd asked a priest once when he visited her father at his real job at the police station), so why was it her duty?

The answer became clear when she attended the twelfth birthday party of her former friend's sibling. The unexpected encounter at Yasmeen's house made the supernatural real, solidifying her path. It was the first time a jinni revealed itself to her.

Severe thunderstorms had forced the girls out of the backyard pool and into the dining room for cake, ice cream and Rukhsana's favorite part, opening gifts. Excited about getting to the good part, she sat down with a piece of pink birthday cake and a plastic fork, careful not to kick over the big red cup of punch sitting precariously near the host's beige area rug.

The house was full of girls, ranging in age from toddlers to their early twenties. They fueled themselves with sugary party foods while the wind swirled wildly through the trees.

The house went dark once or twice while they ate, whipping the younger girls into a state of excitement that forced everyone to shout over their noise. Yasmeen's mother produced extra candles and matches just in case. The younger girls swiped some, using them as makeshift fairy wands.

Beneath the scent of burning wax, something smelled bad. Rukhsana saw a woman lift a toddler and sniff at her diaper, then send her on her way. Cold pool water tickled the back of Rukhsana's neck from her slow-drying hair, causing her to shudder in the cold air. The chill was much too cool for a summer evening.

"Aunty, can you turn off the air conditioner? It's too cold," a young girl complained. The windows rattled and lightning cracked a sickly green across the sky before the power cut off for good. A collective reaction of groans, screams and cheers sent the room buzzing.

The older girls monitored the younger ones, making sure everyone had a partner to navigate them to the bathroom and back again without wandering off through the house and getting into trouble. Most of them stayed put in the party room, intent on seeing the gifts, even if by candlelight. Rukhsana finished her food and tossed everything into a giant black garbage bag in the kitchen, then moved closer to the table.

The birthday girl, Naureen, popular and bubbly since anyone could remember, sat at the table, quiet and unresponsive to the fit of activity around her. Her recent dull personality had been attributed to her father's extended contract at an oil company in Edmonton. The sudden lack of interest in the youth group she attended and the aggressive back-talk to her mother and acting out was easily explained. She missed her dad.

Rukhsana, fifteen at the time, wondered if there was more to it than that. She noticed the faint black outline around the girl at the start of the party but brushed it off as eye strain from her new prescription glasses. Halfway through the party, when she couldn't take it any longer, Rukhsana removed them and watched the afternoon's events unfold through squinted eyes. When the discomfort of eye strain faded, the black aura surrounding Naureen was still there, if not stronger.

As everyone gathered around the table, elongated shadows threw themselves against the wall behind her. Rukhsana tried matching them up to the people standing on the other side of the dancing candlelight, but they didn't look right. She put her glasses back on, then took them off again.

"Girls, don't fight. Naureen will open both of your presents. It doesn't matter which one is opened first," Yasmeen said. "Stand up, Naureen, show everyone your new abaya."

Naureen did them one better. She hopped onto the table and twirled. Girls reacted with nervous laughter. The full skirt of Naureen's abaya flared out as she turned, and Rukhsana wondered if her eyes had played tricks on her when she saw the girl's distorted face.

"Naureen, get down from there," her mother said. Naureen didn't seem to hear. Instead, she hoisted the skirt of her elegant new clothes, revealing her naked body underneath. Once the initial shock set in and everyone shared a collective gasp, Naureen pissed on the gifts, the cake, and in the punch bowl.

Girls shrieked and jumped away from the table. "Did she pee on me? Is it on me?" A girl shrieked, slapping at herself.

"Astaghfirullah, get down right now, Naureen!" Her mortified aunt, easy to embarrass on a good day, leaned over and yanked the hem of the abaya, trying to cover Naureen who fondled herself while perched atop melting urine-soaked gift wrap. "What are you doing? Stop it right now, you disgusting—"

"Get away from me, cunt." A clean sucker punch knocked her aunt out cold. Naureen continued hurling vulgarities at the stunned party-goers and their mothers for the longest minute of their lives.

"Sisters, help me get her down." One brave mother encouraged the others and they grabbed the raging pre-teen, forcing her into the bedroom. They dumped her in a heap on the bed and shut the door behind them. Rukhsana and the older girls rushed to the closed door and listened. Inside, they heard violent flailing and tossing.

"Fix her clothes," someone said. "Hold her down. Hind, Michelle, use those scarves." The girls in the hall listened to the sickening sounds of crunching bones and a deep, distorted laugh, followed by grunting.

"You bitches! I'll haunt your nightmares, I'll possess every one of your kids, you whores. Get away from me, swine!" The demon spat out threats, which some of the women took as promises. The bedroom door opened and closed several times, dwindling the occupants to a dedicated few, including Rukhsana who had slipped inside unnoticed.

By now, the aura burned red at its center with a hint of blue. It took everything they had to tie Naureen's legs. Someone took the initiative to secure her wayward abaya by tying it with scarves. The women prayed over the girl, using the weight of their bodies to keep the bed from knocking against the wall.

While Rukhsana watched, its blazing eyes found her. "We see you.

Did they think that they could hide you forever?" the demon asked. Puzzled, Rukhsana stepped backwards.

"Bismillah. In the name of Allah, leave this body," one of the women said, lightly smacking Naureen's chest and sprinkling Zamzam water on the girl's face. The demon shook with laughter as the women continued their supplications, raising their hands in earnest, seeking forgiveness for the transgressions that had allowed the demon to enter the child. The whites of Naureen's eyes turned crimson as they filled with blood.

Together, the women's voices rose to match the sound of garbled words spewing forth from Naureen's cracked and blistered lips. She hurled harsh, spit-laden epithets at them. Somewhere along the way, spit turned to blood, and Naureen's tongue wagged, nearly tapping her chin. She growled and bit at anyone with the gall to get near her mouth.

Her legs thrashed until the ties came loose and she was able to bear down and defecate on the bed. Someone moved to the bedroom window to release the nauseating smell. "It won't budge!" Outside, the storm raged, growing darker as it whipped through the trees.

"Try harder, I'm gagging!"

"There's more where that came from," the demon taunted.

"Quiet, or I'll knock some sense into you!" Sayyida's mother commanded the jinni.

The jinni glared through Naureen's bloodied eyes at the courageous woman. Rukhsana's blood ran cold. It didn't speak to Sayyida's mother again, but she got its full, glowering attention.

"Nazia, help me open this window," Sayyida's mother commanded. Nazia fit her fingers into the grooves of the window's left side and pulled upward with all her strength, while Sayyida's mother pushed from the top right. Together they strained and managed to open the window.

"Alhamdulillah!" The women shouted their praise. "You did it, Umm Sayyida. Good work, Nazia."

Umm Sayyida nodded. "Thank you, ladies, now, let's focus on the task at hand. We have a child in distress. Hand me something to wedge into this window," she said, sucking in a sharp breath through her open mouth.

A hard gust of wind blew out the candles, leaving everyone in pitch darkness, followed by two quick flashes of lightning. By the time everyone's brains registered the tree trunk crashing through the glass, Umm Sayyida was dead.

Rukhsana stared in horror at the impaled torso of a woman she'd known most of her life. Her mind refused to accept it or make sense of it. After the screaming women vacated the room, Rukhsana, Naureen's jinn-controlled body, and the dead woman remained. She watched the demon admire the wretched results of its work. Rukhsana drew a cup of Zamzam water from the pitcher on the bedside table.

The demon, bored and restless, turned its head in a slow, deliberate manner and rested its eyes upon her. "Let's play."

Rukhsana dipped her fingers into the cup and began. *"Bismillahir Rahmanir Raheem.* In the name of Allah, The Most Gracious, The Most Merciful."

CHAPTER THREE

THE BELL on the front door jingled and a woman entered before Rukhsana could utter a word.

"Excuse me, but we're closed for the night," she warned.

"As Salaamu Alaikum. Are you Sister Rukhsana Davis?"

"Yes, I am."

"My name is Laiba Amin." The woman unwrapped the fluffy scarf from around her mouth and took off her matching hat. Underneath, was a short, olive-skinned woman whose face was framed by a muted pink hijab. White salty streaks stained her cheeks.

"Wa Alaikum As Salaam, sister. What happened? Did someone hurt you? You look upset."

"It's not me who's hurting, Rukhsana. It's my son, Daniyal. He's acting strangely and I think his life is in danger."

Rukhsana withdrew her hands from the epsom salt solution and dried it with a small towel. "Take it easy. Start from the beginning, and tell me everything."

"Things have been going downhill for some time, but I thought Daniyal was acting out because we decided not to move to Chicago. I know he wanted to be near his father, but it's not possible at this time." Laiba readjusted her hijab, wrapping and unwrapping the layers. After the fourth time, she tucked the tail of the fabric inside the folds and fiddled with her purse strap instead.

"What has he done?"

"Well, he's angry all the time, refuses to eat. And he's swearing too. I know some children learn bad behavior outside, but Daniyal only knows well-behaved boys. Anyway, I can't believe that any of them would know the sorts of things he's been saying. Not that he's been playing with them."

"He's not playing with his friends?"

"No. He's withdrawn from everything. He worked so hard to secure a position on the basketball team, and now he doesn't show up for practice."

Rukhsana nodded. "Does he spend a lot of time alone?"

"I think so. I'm an orderly at the hospital, so I'm not with him all the time, but his grandmother is there when I'm not. She says he keeps to himself in his bedroom."

"Does he have access to the internet?"

"Daniyal has one hour of supervised screen time per day. You know what's weird? He doesn't like using the computer anymore, and what's even stranger is that he's forgotten how to turn it on."

"Perhaps he's just out of practice," Rukhsana said.

"I'm not so sure about that, sister. Kids these days know how to use things straight out of the box. It's not just the computer. It's like he's never seen technology before. He sits in his room talking to himself, and sometimes it sounds like there are many voices coming from there."

Rukhsana locked the front door for sure this time, and ushered Laiba to the break room for a cup of tea. She had a feeling it was going to be a while before she left, and wanted them both to feel comfortable. "Please continue, Laiba," she said, putting fresh water in the electric kettle.

"I asked him to make toast this morning, and he couldn't use the toaster. He set the bread inside, then sat there waiting for something to happen. He hadn't pressed the lever. How do you explain that?"

"Tell me more about his behavior," she said, gathering spoons and honey for the tea.

"Sister, he's forgotten how to ride his bike. One minute, his handwriting looks like something a five-year-old would do, then he'll rewrite it with the penmanship of a calligrapher. He either can't spell simple words, or he spells them in the Latin equivalent. He doesn't know Latin!"

"How old is Daniyal?"

"He's twelve."

"Have you taken him to a specialist? It could be a neurological disorder or some other unexplained medical condition."

"We've been to so many doctors, I can't keep letting them poke him with needles and feed him bottles of pills. I'm broke, and the hospital doesn't give us the greatest insurance. Besides, nothing has worked." Laiba accepted a cup of tea and held up her hand. "Before you say anything, I've taken him to six different therapists and they all say he's fine. Alternative medicine, acupuncture, massage therapy, you name it. I also sent him to live with his father for a month."

"What happened?" Rukhsana asked, though she could guess.

"Naseem won't talk about it. From what I could gather, Daniyal ruined some of his expensive clothes. Naseem wanted to punish him. We don't agree on our methods for discipline. He pulled off his belt and attempted to spank Daniyal, but something happened. I had to meet my son and ex-husband at the airport after he'd been gone for only three days. Naseem looked black and blue, and his arm was in a sling. There were belt marks across his face and throat. Sister Rukhsana, Daniyal is small for his age, and Naseem is over two hundred pounds. How could Daniyal have inflicted that much damage?"

Rukhsana nodded and sipped her tea with her right hand while writing with her left. The glass made both hands hurt. "What else is happening?"

"Is that not enough?"

"Please, Laiba, I need to know. Have you noticed any other changes in your home? Smells, temperature fluctuations?"

"Yes to both. Oh, my God, sister. The entire house smells like someone smeared the walls in feces. My son smells so bad, no one will come near him but me and his grandmother."

"Does he need help bathing?"

"I don't want to anymore. I tried to encourage bathing and he did this to me." Laiba rolled up her sleeve and revealed patches of purple bruises. "He's gotten so violent. I don't know how much more I can take. And his grandmother is at risk in our home, but she's got nowhere else to go. I can't send her away." Laiba broke down and cried. Rukhsana got up and fetched a box of tissues for her.

"Here you go," she said, placing the box on the table. She patted Laiba on the back and the woman winced under her touch. More bruises. Rukhsana dropped her hand and returned to her seat at the table. "I'll come out first thing in the morning and give him a thorough examination."

"No, no, you have to come now!" Laiba stood and bumped the table with her thighs, spilling the tea all over. "Oh, no, I'm sorry," she said, reaching for the napkins.

"It's okay, I got it." Rukhsana jumped up and found a roll of paper towels. She mopped up the spilled beverage and made sure there was none on the floor.

"Please, sister. I need you to come tonight. I can pay you extra."

"Absolutely not. My job takes care of my monetary needs. I don't take payment for this."

"Then what will convince you to come?"

Rukhsana shivered from a sudden drop in the room's temperature. The boy had come back. He stood behind Laiba in the doorway of the break room. Rukhsana reached into her sweater pocket and took out the battered mini-sized Quran.

"Let me tell my father that I'll be late, and I'll meet you at your house," she said.

Laiba sighed in relief. "Thank you for this, sister. I don't know how to repay you, but if anyone can administer Allah's healing, it's you, InshaAllah. Your reputation precedes you."

Rukhsana gritted her teeth and darted her eyes towards the boy standing in the doorway. His lips parted as an overly large smile stretched across his face. It grew until she thought his mouth would split at the corners. Instead, they kept stretching until she couldn't bear looking at him. "God willing." She drank her tea. It scalded her throat on the way down, but she kept drinking.

CHAPTER FOUR

RUKHSANA TURNED into Laiba's driveway and cut the engine of her red Honda Accord. She had promised herself never to take on another case with a child, but here she was.

Children were tricky. It took a strong jinni to crack through a child's natural goodness. The clever ones befriended the child, and when that didn't work, they confused them until they were able to penetrate the body. It would take a delicate hand to extract the demon without hurting him. Nothing delighted evil beings more than an innocent soul getting harmed by good intentions.

It wouldn't be easy. It never was. Butterflies twitched in the center of her stomach like it always did before the first visit. As long as she stuck to her routine, she would find her footing and overcome her anxieties.

"Thank you again for coming," Laiba said as Rukhsana climbed out of her vehicle. "I know you've had a long day, but it couldn't wait until morning. He might be dead by then."

Rukhsana stopped in her tracks. "Laiba, don't ever say that again. Allah is with your son."

"Then why won't Allah—"

Rukhsana jerked the woman's arm and pulled her close. "If you're talking like that already, how do you expect to help him? You're his mama, Laiba, toughen up." Laiba broke down into a fit of tears. Rukhsana let the woman go and shook her head. "I'm sorry. I know you must be at wit's end. I shouldn't be harsh like this."

"No," Laiba sniffed. "You're right. I've failed my son, and it's killing me that I can't fix this on my own. My faith is a little shaky."

"It happens to all of us," Rukhsana said. "Now's the time to dig deep. You've seen how devastating evil can be. Let's take care of Daniyal."

"I'll do my best. Come with me, I'll take you inside, Rukhsana."

The women walked up to the porch and climbed the steps. The window at the far left side of the house slammed shut. They heard a fit of laughing from a deep, gravelly voice as they went inside.

"Oh!" Rukhsana, startled by the sharp odors permeating the air, halted just beyond the threshold of the front door and gagged.

"Sorry about the smell, Sister Rukhsana. I tried to air out the house. All the windows are open as you can see, and the air purifiers are going, but they don't help. If you find it unbearable, step outside for a bit." Laiba held the door open.

"No, just give me a second," Rukhsana said through pursed lips. She reached into the black leather bag that she carried, pulling out a box of disposable masks. "I'll wear one of these for now," she said, misting the mask with Zamzam water before she hooked it to her ears. She inhaled and waited for the urge to vomit passed on before stepping further into the house. "Do you want one?"

"No. I'm used to it by now." Laiba closed the door and followed. A thick pile of blankets and two lofty bed pillows sat on the end of the sofa next to a petite woman who slept sitting up. "My mother sleeps in the living room now. She doesn't like to be close to the bedrooms anymore," Laiba explained. "Ma, wake up. We have a guest." Laiba gave the woman a gentle tap on the knee.

The woman stirred, then started to awaken and stared at Rukhsana.

"Salaam. Are you a nurse?" The woman asked, pointing at the mask and medical bag.

"Wa Alaikum As Salaam. Yes, I'm a nurse, among other things," Rukhsana replied.

"Rukhsana, this is my mother, Mariya. Rukhsana is the exorcist I was telling you about, Ma." Laiba motioned for Rukhsana to sit in an armchair next to the sofa. "She's going to take a look at Daniyal and see if she can help him."

"InshaAllah," Rukhsana said. "I'll need to do a full evaluation, medical and spiritual," she said.

"Have you done this before?" Mariya asked, sitting up. Rukhsana noticed the plastic bag of ice propped under her ankle, which looked swollen and bruised.

"Yes, many times. Would you like me to take a look at that?" Rukhsana nodded in the direction of her ankle.

"No. I already went to the clinic down the street this morning. They told me to keep it wrapped up, but I needed to loosen the bandage for a bit. It cuts off my circulation," Mariya said.

Rukhsana approached the woman and knelt to look at her ankle. "It should remain bandaged. I can rewrap it for you," Rukhsana offered, taking the woman's foot in her hands and gently rotating it.

"Thank you," Mariya said. Tears welled in her eyes and Laiba handed her a tissue.

"Did Daniyal do this to you?"

"Yes. I was making the bed and he got free and squeezed my ankle so hard with his hand, I thought he was going to break it. The doctor said there's a sprain and lots of bruising, but otherwise it should be fine with a little pain medication and elevation."

Rukhsana reached into her medical bag and pulled out a fresh roll of compression bandages. "Are you two the only adults in the home?"

"Yes," Laiba said. "My parents are divorced. Daniyal's grandfather wants nothing to do with us. He came over for a visit to assess the situation for himself and blamed us for Daniyal's condition. He told me not to contact him again, and he left."

"Have the police ever become involved when Daniyal has gotten violent? Is there a record of abuse with the authorities?" Rukhsana asked, wrapping the ankle.

"No. I lied to them, to protect Laiba's job. If the doctors saw this place, they'd be horrified." Mariya said. "I told them that I fell, but if you look closely, you can clearly see his small handprints. It's too shameful to talk about in public, Rukhsana. How do you tell people that your grandson is beating you up? I feel like I've failed him," she said. "I don't know how much longer any of us can last. I feel like he's becoming a monster. Maybe his grandfather is right. We've done something wrong and Allah is punishing us through Daniyal." The older woman buried her face in her hands and cried.

"Stop it, Ma. It's not our fault," Laiba said.

Rukhsana watched the women console one another, clutched in a desperate embrace. She nodded to herself, thankful that they had a sense of solidarity in the household. Often, the infighting caused by the possession was harder on the family than the possession itself. This didn't seem to be the case in Laiba's home, which Rukhsana took as a positive sign.

She glanced around the house, looking for anything that might explain the possession. Often talismans were the culprit. Nothing stood out. She'd check under the child's bed when she entered the bedroom.

"You must think we're insane," Laiba said, wiping her eyes.

"No. I don't think that at all. Dealing with this situation must be anxiety-inducing in ways that I can't fathom."

Somewhere in the back of the house, laughter started up again. "Did you girls bring me a fresh whore to play with? She doesn't smell fresh, but I'll fuck her anyway." Laiba clenched her jaw and her mother slumped deeper into the sofa.

"SubhanAllah," Mariya said.

"Oh my God, I'm so sorry about that," Laiba said, grabbing hold of Rukhsana's hand.

Rukhsana winced. She took out her Quran and kissed it, then rose from her chair. "I'd like to see Daniyal now."

CHAPTER FIVE

THE STENCH MADE her eyes water as she worked her way through the oppressive air. She'd once entered a home with twenty cats in the basement, but that didn't come close to this. She used her cellphone's flashlight to navigate, bouncing the light off the walls and Laiba's back.

The condition of the house worsened as they made their way down the hall. Dirty cobwebs clung from the corners of the ceiling in front of the boy's room like Halloween decorations, and thick spirals of black mold spread from the doorway outwards. Something scurried over her foot, making her thankful that she hadn't removed her shoes.

Laiba knocked on the last door at the end of the hall. "Daniyal, you've got a visitor. Give Miss Rukhsana a proper greeting." Rukhsana peered through a gaping hole in the wall that allowed her to see inside the bedroom. She felt an eerie presence though she saw no one.

Laiba gripped the doorknob to her son's bedroom and opened it. She leaned in a little and smiled an apology at Rukhsana. It was obvious that she didn't want to go inside. Rukhsana didn't blame her. She heard a crackling sound as warm air from the hall collided with the cold air around the door frame. Her instincts told her to grab Laiba by the hand, collect Mariya, then leave this place and never return. She took a deep breath and entered the bedroom.

Rukhsana craned her neck, looking for signs of life in the slim shape under the covers. Daniyal lay there, stiff as a board. Her flashlight flickered. Rukhsana had a sneaking suspicion that he had been waiting for them.

Adjusting to the dark, she focused on a pair of long chain handcuffs that wrapped around the headboard and disappeared under the covers. An IV drip sat on a stand next to the bed; its tubes also ran beneath the blanket. She reached over and flipped the light switch to get a better look.

"It doesn't work. The electrical outlets are fine, and the wiring is okay too, but nothing lights up in here like it's supposed to," Laiba explained as she entered the room. "The jinni has full control now." She pulled a candle from the nightstand and lit it with a lighter she produced from the pocket of her abaya, then handed it to Rukhsana and stepped back into the hall.

"Thank you," Rukhsana said. She walked around familiarizing herself with the layout of the room. There was nothing to indicate a child lived here. No toys, no decorative posters. No school books or sports equipment. Even the closets were bare.

"We've emptied the room of things that he could use as a weapon," Laiba said, reading her mind.

"Does he hurt himself?"

"Sometimes. He used to rip out the feeding tube before we started handcuffing him. I know it looks archaic, but I want to make sure he's safe from himself, you know? The medical restraints don't hold as well as these do. I couldn't get any more from the hospital without looking like I was running an illegal clinic anyway. You know how it is. They blame us orderlies for everything that goes missing."

"Our little secret," Rukhsana said.

Laiba nodded. "Thanks."

"Does Daniyal have allergies or medical conditions I should know about?"

"He's got asthma. There hasn't been a flare-up since this started though."

"I see you have an IV attached. Does he have someone looking after him or did you administer this on your own?"

"I did it with Doctor Muhammad's approval. My mother is a long-retired nursing assistant, and her eyesight isn't what it used to be, but it's still handy having her care in a situation like this, isn't it?"

"It is," Rukhsana agreed.

"The problem isn't completely medical though. I can only attach feeding tubes and hydrate him, but I can't stop whatever's causing it." Laiba gestured towards the unmoving body shrouded in the blanket.

"You've got a lot on your plate right now. Why don't you sit with your mom and take a break?"

"Are you sure that's a good idea? I mean, he's dangerous. You've seen what he's done to us."

"It's alright, Laiba. I'll call you if I need you."

"Holler and I'll come." She shot Rukhsana a look that was a mixture of concern and relief.

"Do you have more candles? I prefer not working in total darkness."

"Sure, but be careful, or he'll burn down the house. He's tried before."

"I'm sure we'll be fine."

"Alright, I'll get them for you."

Laiba brought in two trays aligned with pillar candles of varying lengths. She placed one tray on the far side of the room and lit each candle. When she finished, she left the lighter on the tray, and thanked Rukhsana again before closing the door.

Here we go. Rukhsana raised her hands and whispered a prayer, protecting herself from the evils in the seen and unseen, and one for Daniyal. When she finished, she lowered her hands and watched the still body in the bed. She wondered how the jinni would show itself. It was always something dramatic.

She crossed her legs and folded her hands in her lap. The stillness of the room felt thick and oppressive, but she waited. Rukhsana listened to the faint sound of a ticking clock. It sounded worlds away, rather than at the end of the hall.

The steady rhythm brought her comfort, and she practiced a meditation technique that she learned at a conference a few years ago, visualizing her heart beating in cadence to the clock. Slowing down and being in the moment. Scary as it was, she needed to be present—aware of every detail.

She reached into her bag and pulled out the essentials. Squirt gun full of Zamzam water. Stethoscope. Tape recorder. Two-way radio. She glanced at the scar tissue on the back of her right hand that still gave her pain, six years later. Rukhsana found out the hard way that you should never take writing instruments to an exorcism. She picked up the tape recorder and voiced a quick note to herself. "Bring a battery-powered lantern to the next session."

The body, of course, had moved to the other side of the bed while she unpacked her tools. *It wants to play.* Daniyal lay there, wrapped up like he had been, but shifted more to the left side of the bed. She could have passed it off as a trick of the mind, but the IV tube and handcuff chains pulled taut, at a hard, forty-five degree angle. Daniyal's face remained obscured, his body mummified by the thick blue and red patchwork quilt. She breathed in and out deeply, an empathetic reflex. *It must be stuffy under there.* He offered a muffled giggle.

The temperature dropped further. Steam rose from her nose and lips. She shivered against the cold and wished she was someplace warm in the deep South like Charleston or Houston.

Rukhsana had been meaning to travel for some time, but hadn't had a chance to go far. Too many people depended on her. She glanced at the corner of a white envelope peeking out of the bag and shoved it back inside. *Don't think about it now. Focus on the boy.*

She glanced at the bed again. Still playing around, the demon had shifted the boy's body to the right side of the bed, tubes and chains leaning. *I looked away for a second. How could he move from one side of the bed to the other that fast without making a sound? Pay attention.*

Rukhsana got out of her head and got to work. She patted the tiny Quran in her pocket and began to recite by memory. Three years of full time memorization of the Arabic text as a child and a lifetime of review made the words as natural as brushing her teeth. She started with the opening surah. Might as well begin at the beginning. See what she was working with.

"Audhubillahi min ash shaytan ir rajeem. Bismillah ar-Rahman ar-Raheem. In the name of Allah, Most Gracious, Most Merciful..." she continued in Arabic. The body stirred. She rocked herself off the chair, rising to her full height as she continued reciting. The chains moved back and forth, rattling against the headboard.

"Praise be to Allah, the Cherisher and Sustainer of the worlds." Her feet inched closer to the edge of the bed. "Most Gracious, Most Merciful. Master of the Day of Judgment."

The body stirred, creating a ripple effect in the blanket. "Thee do we worship and Thine aid we seek." Daniyal's body trembled under the covers. She hadn't expected such a strong reaction this early, considering how far gone things seemed. They made the demon sound strong, way stronger than this. Either the family had exaggerated how powerful the jinni was, or it was putting on quite the show.

"Show us the straight way," she continued. The bed trembled, bumping back and forth between the matching nightstands. A tingling sensation traveled up her spine. Something felt off.

"The way of those on whom Thou hast bestowed Thy Grace, those whose portion is not wrath, and who go not astray." Rukhsana's shin bumped the mattress and the bed went still.

Now, she would get a good look at him and see how bad it was. This first part was the hardest. Facing off with a malevolent force. A chunk of her heart always broke when she searched for a sign of humanity in the victim's eyes and found none. She wondered where the innocent went when the demons took over; no one had given her a satisfying answer yet. But she kept asking, again and again. A quote skimmed the surface of her mind. Something about going mad from doing the same thing but expecting a different result. She brushed the mocking words away. After all, wasn't she already out of her mind for being here? Who else would voluntarily shut themselves in with a monster?

Rukhsana reached down and tugged at a corner of the blanket. It didn't come free easily, so she used both hands and gave it a hard pull. It was wound tighter than she thought. She leaned in to give it another tug, this time, pulling it free. Rukhsana felt a sharp tap on her right shoulder and started. She turned around and faced the grayish-brown pus-filled face smiling up at her.

"Daniyal? How? I don't understand." Rukhsana glanced from the boy to the covered body in the bed.

"Surprise," the boy said. "Shapeshifting hurts, you know. Stretching the bones, changing the body to resemble someone else's. But the look on your face is worth it."

Movement near the door caught her eye and Rukhsana turned to see Mariya standing in the hallway. Her face was twisted into a gruesome smile that ran Rukhsana's blood cold.

"Mariya? What's going on?" *Why does she look like that?* Rukhsana gulped. Deep down, she already knew. The demons had pulled the wool over her eyes.

Daniyal grabbed the covers and yanked them free from the bed.

Rukhsana stared at the bed in horror. "Laiba." She saw the emaciated cadaver lying on the bed, still caught in a death scream. The torso had been eaten away by the biggest maggots she had ever seen in her life. "Inna lillahi wa inna ilayhi rajioon."

"Your God doesn't care about you, Rukhsana," the demon inside Mariya said. "You're going to Hell with us, but in the meantime, let's try to have a little fun."

CHAPTER SIX

RUKHSANA CLUTCHED the Quran in her pocket and tried not to panic. The little boy stared at her from his perch on an empty bookcase across the room. She listened to her erratic breathing and wondered what to do next. The other demon possessing Daniyal's grandmother stayed by the bedroom door, blocking the possibility of escape. She remembered that there was a bathroom behind her. She hoped the door had a lock.

"You should have seen the look on your stupid whore face when you uncovered that dead pig," Daniyal said. "I haven't had this much fun in ages."

Outnumbered, all she could think to do was appeal to the boy. He had to be in there somewhere. "Daniyal. This is Miss Rukhsana. I'm a friend of your mother's. Terrible things have happened, but I'm here for you. You've got to fight the jinni. Ask Allah for help."

"He can't hear you, stupid. I've taken over his young, growing body and I'm going to stay inside until he's become a rotten old man. Imagine the chaos I'll cause once I've gotten him into the prison system."

"Or, an asylum," the possessed older woman said from the doorway. Rukhsana glanced from one to the other, horrified. She pitied them, as they were both frail for their ages, and had no doubt been easier to contaminate. How long had the demons been in control of their bodies? She knew that the longer they remained, the worse the outcome.

Calm down. Keep your wits. This is what you signed up for. She took a deep breath and listened for the clock in the hall. Tick. Tock. Tick. Tock. The metronomic lull brought her back to reality and she pushed down her fear.

There was nothing she could do for poor Laiba, but she could try saving her mother and son. She took a deep breath and began reciting.

"Alif, Laam, Meem." The young boy's contorted face belied the confidence of the demon's words with a subtle twitch. It was all Rukhsana needed. She continued reciting from the surah as she took baby steps towards her black bag.

"Shut up, you bitch. No one wants to hear that!" Mariya shrieked, tearing at her hair.

Rukhsana picked up the two-way radio. "As Salaamu Alaikum. Abi, this is Rukhsana, over." She turned up the volume and kept reciting as she waited for her father.

She took a breath and checked the jinn. Mariya had dropped to her knees, Daniyal had not. He sat watching through his dead eyes. She could almost see him calculating what to do next.

Rukhsana edged along the foot of the bed and swiped the squirt gun filled with Zamzam water. She kept an eye on Daniyal as she moved towards Mariya.

"As Salaamu Alaikum. Hello? Rukhsana, is that you?" her father asked on the other end of the radio.

"Wa Alaikum As Salaam, Abi. Need your help."

"Where are you?"

"You know Sister Laiba, right? I'm at her house." Rukhsana squirted Mariya with the holy water and she let out a blood-curdling screech.

"Are you performing ruqya? Rukhsana, we talked about this."

"Abi, please, not now! Do you know where she lives?"

"Yes, I'm familiar with the neighborhood. I'll find you."

She glanced at Daniyal. He hadn't made a move. Mariya squirmed on the floor and covered her face with her hands. Rukhsana wretched from the smell of burning flesh. It was working. She squeezed the trigger again and tried to keep her stomach contents under control.

Her father came back on the radio. "I looked it up. She's on Cinnamon Street?"

"Yes. House nine-thirteen. Can you come over? I've got two cases and a body."

"Bodies? I'm calling for a squad car," her father said. She could hear his squeaky office chair when he stood and grabbed his keys. "I'm on my way, Roxie. Be careful."

"Abi, hurry."

CHAPTER SEVEN

THEY WERE AT A STALEMATE, each side sizing up one another, testing the boundaries and looking for weak spots. Rukhsana kept at it, using the Zamzam water and reciting the holy scripture, pressing forward at the end of each verse, getting closer to Daniyal. He sat and watched.

A low snarl began at the back of his throat, increasing in volume and cadence until his small Adam's apple rattled like a mini jackhammer, sounding like a cross between a wolf and a diesel engine. Rukhsana pretended not to hear the noise emanating from him. She paused her recitations to keep an eye on Mariya, who hadn't moved after Rukhsana sprayed her with the squirt gun.

She lay still on the floor, in the same position. *I don't trust that. They fooled me once but I'm not letting it happen again.*

She left her for now and focused on Daniyal. "Leave this body, shaytaan. Return to your realm, and forget about this place," Rukhsana said.

"I'm never leaving!" A flash of anger passed through the cold, dead-looking eyes of the boy. Rukhsana waited for him to retaliate, but he didn't move. He sat on the dresser, watching her place one foot in front of the other in measured steps.

"Leave!" Rukhsana shot Daniyal with the squirt gun and he

screeched loud enough to give her pause, lest she stress the boy's body too much. She made a mental note to check his vitals as soon as she had the chance. The last thing a raaqi should do is risk the life of their client by ignoring the needs of the body. There was enough negative press about imams and so-called exorcists who beat people to death in the name of healing. They didn't stick to the code. Mercy before expulsion.

Although Daniyal's face broke out in beads of sweat, he shivered in the cold room. At least his body was responding to the environment. But why hadn't he tried to fight harder? What was he waiting for?

Outside, the sound of cars pulling into the rocky driveway made Rukhsana stand a little straighter. Someone had arrived. The unmistakable grumble of her father's old cruiser and another car. The possessed boy's eyes gleamed in the headlights as they shone through the window. It was her turn to shiver.

He wants an audience.

She heard a knock at the front door and the jiggle of the handle. "Hello? Rukhsana? Are you here?"

"Salaam Abi, I'm in the room at the back." She glanced at the doorway. Mariya was gone. She stepped backwards at an angle, keeping Daniyal in her sight line and looked for her. *Shoot.* Mariya's body now lay sprawled on the bed next to that of her deceased daughter. They both appeared dead.

"Rukhsana?"

"In here, Abi." The door opened wider and Rukhsana let out an audible sigh when her father stepped inside. Appearing tense and wary, her father glanced at her, a hint of anger lingering beneath the surface. She knew he'd never let her hear the end of it later. Chief Davis did not want his daughter performing exorcisms, and as far as he was concerned, her going behind his back was the biggest offense.

"Astaghfirullah," he said, noticing the women. "Both dead?" He tried the light switch on the wall, then took out a pen flashlight from his uniform shirt.

"No. One deceased. One possessed. Hey, Officer Marlon. Officer Pike." The men stepped into the room and immediately began gagging.

"What the hell is going on in this place, Chief? It stinks like a rotten corpse in here," Officer Marlon said. He stuck his face into the opening of his jacket to counter the smell with the scent of his body.

"That's what we're here to find out, Jake," her father said. Jake Marlon tried the light switch next to the bed then took out his flashlight.

"Hey, Rukhsana. Are you okay?" Officer Pike glanced from Rukhsana to the bed then back at her. His face had gone green.

"I'm good." She shuddered a little as the temperature in the room dropped.

"What about him? Did he get hurt?" Officer Marlon pointed at Daniyal with his flashlight. Rukhsana followed the beam and found the boy had changed positions.

He was sitting on a chair now, his legs pulled close to his chest. His body rocked back and forth and tears ran down his smooth baby face. Any evidence of a jinni tampering with his body was gone. Had Rukhsana arrived when her father and his officers had, it would have fooled them all.

"It's complicated," Rukhsana said.

"Any idea how they died?" Chief Davis asked his daughter.

Officer Marlon moved closer to the bed to inspect the bodies of the women. "Looks like they've been deceased for some time," he said.

"The one nearer to me is not dead, Jake." Rukhsana stressed. "Be careful."

Officer Marlon shined his flashlight at the bed. "No offense, Rukhsana, but I've seen a body or two in my day. She looks stone cold dead to me."

"We've been through this a thousand times, Jake. I don't call you to a scene unless something unusual is happening."

"And there's always been a logical explanation as far as I'm concerned, Rukhsana. You and your father have some seriously active imaginations."

"Knock it off, Jake," Officer Pike said. "I can vouch for the chief and his daughter. I've seen plenty of things that have kept me up at night."

"Thank you, Chris," Rukhsana said. "Now, back to it. The deceased woman is Laiba Amin. The woman next to her is her mother, Mariya—

careful Abi." Rukhsana watched her father lean in close to Mariya to study her face. He placed a hand on her neck in search of a pulse.

"I'm not getting anything, sweetie. Maybe she succumbed a few minutes ago," he said. "I'm going to need you to explain to me how these people ended up dead."

"Look out, Chief!" Officer Pike reached for his taser. The light from Officer Marlon's flashlight hit Mariya's face. Her eyes were opened wide as she pounced on the chief. She flipped him with an inhuman amount of strength, pinning him beneath her on the bed.

"Abi!" Rukhsana rushed to aid her father, but Daniyal was faster. He jumped on her back, pulling her hijab, jerking her head backwards until it snapped. She lost her balance and hit the corner of the bed. She saw stars as she rolled onto the floor. Officer Pike leaped over the bed, landing in the space beside her and the boy.

He grabbed the boy's shoulders and Daniyal sent him flying with an effortless backhand, knocking him into the corner of the night table.

"Pike," Rukhsana said. The officer lay still, unresponsive. Daniyal turned his attention back to Rukhsana, yanking her off the floor and pushing her over the edge of the bed onto her stomach. He sat on the backs of her thighs and ripped at her clothing, tearing the abaya into strips. Another rip and he was through her t-shirt. The band of her bra popped, and the sensation of ice digging into her flesh made her cry out in agony.

Rukhsana pressed her face deep into the soiled mattress, blinded by the pain. The jinni's heavy, distorted laugh boomed in her ears. Beyond the pain and the laughter, she heard her father's cry above her own. She lifted her head enough to replace the burning air in her lungs. The slight movement was enough to see what was happening to her father.

The demon inside Mariya presented itself, morphing the tiny woman's face. Her hands elongated and sharpened at the tips. She brought them down against the chief's face, slicing skin down to the bone.

"Help him!" Rukhsana managed. Officer Marlon stood with his taser in hand, stunned at the scene. He watched the chief scream in agony under the writhing, slashing demon and he glanced equally in horror at the small boy as he pressed Rukhsana's face in the mattress, smothering her while he tore at the rest of her clothing. Rukhsana felt the boy's icy legs dig into the backs of her exposed thighs. She felt hard, cold flesh press against her own. Somewhere along the way, he'd removed his pants.

Officer Marlon took a step forward and stopped cold when the demon's eyes met his. "I can stick it in you next, Jake. Wait your turn," the demon said, waving his erection at the officer. Officer Marlon backed away until he hit the wall. His bladder let go, creating a cloud of steam around his lower half.

"That's a good boy," Daniyal's jinni said, delighted to have so many audience members. "I can't wait to take care of this bitch, then move on to you, pig. I told you, girl. I was gonna have you. Just like I had that one over there. You should have seen the look on her face. But first, let's see your daddy get a special kiss!"

The jinni pulled the back of Rukhsana's head, bending her spine in a painful arc. The other jinni held her father's bleeding face between its hands, forcing his mouth open from the vise-like grip. Mariya opened her mouth, then leaned into him, emptying a bloody stream of stomach contents, bile and whatever else into his open lips. She locked her mouth over him and Rukhsana could see her father's throat rippling, taking something inside.

"Beautiful," Daniyal's jinni said. "Now, he's one with us. Your turn, whore!" Several shots rang out and Rukhsana felt the demon's body go slack and collapse on top of hers. She tried to squirm her way out from under him but couldn't move.

Officer Pike groaned and raised himself up to a kneeling position, using the mattress for leverage as he pointed the gun at Mariya. "Move away from him or you're next. I'm not kidding! Move!" The demon let the chief go, allowing him to collapse onto the bed.

"M-move!" Officer Marlon's shaky hands wrapped his service revolver and he joined his partner. Mariya's grin widened in a way that made Rukhsana's stomach turn.

"Well, look who's found his nerve," the jinni said in a distorted, raspy voice. "I thought you were going to stand there pissing yourself while we finished the others, but look at you, protecting and serving like a good little pig. Now, I'm going to rip your heart out and feed it to you," she said.

"That's enough. Move," Officer Pike said. His body wobbled and he stumbled from the sudden shift in gravity as he stood. He pulled the boy off Rukhsana and flung her tattered clothing across her backside.

Slowly, she slid off the bed holding the back of her abaya closed. The ache in her heart for the boy and his mother rivaled the pain she felt in her body. It was a shame that she hadn't been able to help them. She hoped the officers could calm Mariya and prevent her from hurting herself or them.

"I want you to get off the bed, nice and easy, lady. Don't try anything, or I'll end you right now," Officer Pike said. "Jake, get your cuffs out."

"What? Why can't you cuff her? I'll cover you."

"Don't worry, man. If she tries any shit, I've got my eye on her."

Officer Marlon reached for his cuffs and edged forward, careful not to slip in the puddle of piss at his feet. "Alright, Miss. I'm going to cuff you now so that you don't hurt yourself. Can you lay down on the bed for me?"

Rukhsana found it absurd that he'd try to reason with her. It. The thing on the bed hardly looked human anymore with its stretched out appendages and talons.

Mariya snarled at him and dropped to her hands and knees on the mattress. She began barking, sounding a lot like the real thing. Officer Marlon hesitated, tossing an unsure glance at his partner.

"Go on, Jake. You got this."

"Shut up, Chris. You're not the one doing this and you damn sure aren't helping."

"Sorry. I'm trying to encourage you."

"Yeah, well, I already pissed myself, so nothing you say is gonna help right now." He watched Mariya's tongue grow and loll from her lips, which were changing into something awful and snout-like.

Rukhsana backed away from the bed. This didn't look good at all. People didn't morph into other creatures, did they? She wondered how things had gotten so out of control? Had she suspected anything outside of an ordinary exorcism, she would have brought her father in the first place.

Sure, the chief was out of practice, and all but happy about performing them, but he could have helped her get the upper hand instead of whatever was happening right now.

She glanced at her father's unresponsive body. Whatever the jinni had done to him could be reversed. It always could. She looked at Daniyal's cold body. Almost always.

"Hurry up, Jake, she's... Back it up lady! I'm warning you." Officer Pike scrambled backward as the woman on the bed no longer resembled anything of human origin. Her face, long and toothy, sprouted long, dark hairs that extended down her shoulders. Her fingers shrank and became closer together, the palms rounding themselves into padded feet. Her legs, now very furry and dog-like, burst from the pants she wore.

"Chris, just shoot her. Please, I can't... I don't understand what's happening." Officer Marlon backed away from the bed as the dog-woman threatened him with her deep growls, promising pain.

"I won't kill her, I'll just— Officer Pike's weapon discharged twice as Mariya pounced. The first bullet hit Laiba's corpse. The second buried itself in Officer Marlon's forehead, exiting in a dark, wet splash on the wall behind him. "Christ! Jake, I'm sorry, I—" The dead policeman toppled over, and Rukhsana shrank into herself, unable to handle the vicious tearing sound coming from Officer Pike's throat.

On the floor, near the tipped-over nightstand, she found discarded items from her bag. There was a bottle of black seed oil and a thermos of Zamzam water in case she needed to refill the squirt gun. She quickly untwisted the cap of the thermos and got to her feet.

"Bismillah." Rukhsana threw the contents of the thermos on the dog-woman and prayed it did some good. The creature howled in dismay and pain, snapping its jaws at no one in particular. The head of the creature snapped forward, searching for Rukhsana. She stepped backwards, conscious of the wall and the window directly behind her. The creature began to sway back and forth, stalking its new victim. It stepped on top of Officer Pike's dead body and watched Rukhsana's futile attempt to escape. It stepped closer to the edge of the bed, letting the officer's body fall to the floor near Daniyal's.

"In the name of Allah, Most Gracious, Most Merciful," Rukhsana began. She had to try, there was no other option. Fear and panic rose in her throat, making her voice waver, but she dug deep into her memory and pulled out a surah that she hadn't recited in some time. The words stumbled out in a clumsy, chopped up fashion from rustiness and fright, but once she got going, they became clear and her confidence grew.

The creature chomped at the air, trying to get closer to her, waiting for its chance. She kept reciting, not allowing any time for the demon to conjure a clever attack. Rukhsana didn't want to know what else it could become. With each death, the creature seemed to grow in strength and ingenuity. She couldn't allow it to feed off of her. Killing a raaqi like herself would enhance its power, making it harder to defeat.

She took another cautious step backward, leaving a wide space between her and the jinni. After weighing her options, she decided it didn't make sense to make a run for it. Why run? The devil loved a good chase. It was a fight they couldn't stand. Rukhsana squared up her shoulder and recited louder. The creature winced then growled a warning at her. She paid it no heed.

The words flowed from her lips entrancing her, entering her veins, filling them with an other-worldly supercharged power. She felt lighter, yet steeled by the resolve in the words spilling from her mouth. The creature snarled and barked at her, foam dripping from its jowls. It was fully formed now, its body lit by the discarded flashlights of the policemen; hairy, sleek, and blacker than the shadows.

Her father stirred on the bed behind it. He was conscious now, holding his Glock in his hand. Rukhsana cleared her throat and recited louder as she leapt forward a bit, to keep the creature's attention locked on her. When she was sure the blacks of its eyes were trained on her, she picked up the squirt gun and sent an arc of holy water towards it. Drops of water rained down its back, sloughing off chunks of fur and skin as it went. The demon's hind legs shifted in anticipation, and she knew the time had come.

It lunged at her with everything it could muster. Had her father discharged his gun first, or did the creature launch itself at her before shots were fired? It didn't matter. It all happened so fast, Rukhsana barely had time to block her face and throat with a forearm. When the creature clamped its jaws around her, she reached under the body with her free hand. She made the lightest form of contact, sweeping the creature up and over her through the air.

She did a half-flip through the air with her forearm still in the mouth of the monster. Her father shot again, bullets whizzing by her, too close for comfort. The bullets lodged themselves in the creature's flesh as it crashed through the window.

It let go of Rukhsana, ripping her arm as it fell into the bushes outside the bedroom. She hit the floor with her knees, then crawled to the window. Beyond the broken panes of glass, the creature, hurt, but not dead, rose to its feet. Before her eyes, the canine again morphed into a human form. Rukhsana watched a pale white woman in a red dress run off into the night. Rukhsana heard her laughing like a hyena.

Behind her, she heard her father's gun clicking and clicking. She saw his reflection in the window. He was aiming it at her back.

CHAPTER EIGHT

"LISTEN RUKHSANA, I need you to explain it to me one more time. What were you doing at the residence?"

Rukhsana watched the solid frame of Detective D'Angelo Wright pace back and forth in front of her hospital bed. *If he keeps this up, he's going to wear a hole in the floor.*

D'Angelo was one of the six detectives employed by the small station outside of Salem, Virginia. Four, now that Pike and Marlon were dead. One of the others was on loan to another small town, and the last two were on maternity leave. He took on their caseloads and managed to solve more than half by their second trimesters.

Officer Rosa West stood near the door, watching. The two women couldn't be any more opposite. Rosa was short with long brownish-red hair and hazel eyes. Rukhsana's complexion was dark brown, on the taller side with long, thick cornrows, which neither had ever seen. Officer West went everywhere the detective went if it were possible.

Now that her father was out of commission, D'Angelo had stepped up, herding the press and calling in help from nearby stations who had officers to spare. D'Angelo always stepped up. Rumor had it that his true reason for being indispensable to the chief was proving himself worthy of Rukhsana's affections. She pretended not to have heard the gossip.

"It's like I told you, D'Angelo. I stopped by the house to check up on the family. They've been having issues with... they've had spiritual difficulties."

"And you were there to talk to the mother and you said, the grandmother, Mariya... What's her last name?"

"I don't know. I had never met her before today. I came to the house under the pretense that Laiba's son, Daniyal, needed spiritual guidance."

Detective Wright stopped pacing and faced her. His dark eyes looked onto hers. "And what happened when you got there?"

"I sat on the sofa and spoke with Mariya, then I went to the boy's bedroom."

"You didn't notice the smell?"

"The whole place reeked, detective. But I didn't realize there was a dead body in the house. I just thought... I don't know what I thought."

"You didn't realize? Really? Rukhsana, you're a nurse and dead bodies are the worst smell in the world. You didn't know?" Detective Wright frowned at her.

She had the urge to tell him more, to let him in on the dark secrets that plagued her, but she couldn't explain what happened in a way that he'd believe. Besides, she'd gotten enough people killed. It was best if she kept him out of the loop.

Detective Wright sat in the bedside chair and leaned his big brown forearms on the bed rail. "Rukhsana, I know there's something you're not telling me. But we've been here before, haven't we? Weird things happen to you, people get hurt, your father swoops in to save the day and fill out the reports. I'm not here to judge you. I'm a friend and I want to help, but this time, things are really out of hand. Two good cops are dead, and your father's lying in a hospital bed in a catatonic state. For once in your life, woman, will you tell me the truth?"

"Nothing happened, D'Angelo. Nothing I could explain in a way that makes sense," she said. "If you want to help me, you'll try to find Mariya." *If she's back to her normal self.* A chill ran down her spine. *What if that was her normal self?*

"See, that's the thing, Rukhsana. There is no Mariya."

Rukhsana put down the small carton of apple juice the nurse had given her and readjusted herself on the bed. The bandages were sealed to her back and forearm, making it awkward to move. Thanks to the morphine drip, D'Angelo was starting to not make sense. "What do you mean?"

"Well, for starters, Daniyal doesn't have a grandmother named Mariya. In fact, both his grandmothers are deceased."

Rukhsana stopped fiddling with the bed controls. "But, I met her. She was the one I talked to." She sank into the bed, winced, and sat up again. "I consoled her."

"I think you have to accept the fact that this person may have been preying on members of the community. Perhaps she forced her way inside the home, killed the mother and forced the kid to keep quiet. It could explain why he was acting out."

"Oh, he was acting out, alright," Rukhsana said, adjusting the bed.

"I can't believe they shot him though. He was just a little kid. Did he really do that to you?"

"You're the cop, D'Angelo. Can't your forensics guys clear this up?"

"They will. I've got someone matching the skin fragments under his nails to your DNA as we speak."

"Okay, good," she said. "What about Mariya—or whoever she is?"

"We didn't find any evidence of another woman at the scene, Rukhsana."

"How could you not? She did something to my father. He was fine before she attacked him. I saw it with my own eyes."

"Rukhsana, I'm sure you saw something, but I think you might be confused."

"What about Officer Pike?"

"His injuries are conducive to a dog attack and we have animal control looking for it. But we don't have anything linking a woman to the scene."

"A dog?" she asked.

"Yes, which you failed to mention. Wanna tell me about it? Where was the canine in this story you've concocted?"

Rukhsana shook her head. She knew they wouldn't find anything. They were looking for a rabid dog, not a possessed senior citizen or a young woman in a red dress. What was that about? "What about Laiba? How did she die?"

"Don't know yet. It looks like she suffered from sexual assault and had a heart attack."

Rukhsana's stomach dropped and she wretched.

"Whoa, do you need this?" D'Angelo placed the kidney-shaped vomit tray under her chin and helped her lean forward.

"Thank you," she said, dry-heaving over it. "I'm alright." She pushed the tray away from her and took in deep gulps of air.

"We're gonna figure this out together, Rukhsana. I'll keep you posted if we find her."

"What about my dad? Have you gone to see him? Is he responding?"

"I haven't, but I heard they're doing everything they can to make the chief comfortable. Did the doctor tell you how long they're keeping you here?"

"I can leave in the morning if my stitches look good."

"I think you should stay as long as you need to," he said. "You've been through a traumatic experience. If you need to talk to someone, I can have the department therapist get in touch with you."

"Thanks, but no thanks. I don't need a therapist."

"Normally, I would suggest your father since he used to be an imam..." he trailed off.

"Right."

"Maybe you could talk to a different imam since the chief isn't able to help you right now."

"Maybe," she shrugged, instantly regretting the motion. D'Angelo saw the pain on her face and stepped closer, unsure how to help.

"Are you in pain? What can I do?" He reached out and touched her shoulder but drew back when she flinched.

"How's it going in here, Rukhsana? Did you manage to get the juice down?" Nurse Sheila Randall knocked on the door and entered the room.

"Hey, Sheila. I couldn't finish it."

"Nauseous?" The nurse asked, washing her hands at the sink.

"Yes."

"Poor baby. Is the morphine at least helping with your pain?" Nurse Randall asked, grabbing Rukhsana's wrist and laying it against her hip with one hand while the other wrapped the blood pressure cuff around her arm.

"It's alright. I'm not crazy about it though."

"Bad dreams?"

"Not yet, but I know they'll come as soon as I go to sleep." Rukhsana wasn't looking forward to them. Demons had always chased her during sleep after an exorcism. It was the perfect time for them to wear her down without suffering damage from her defensive tactics.

"Your blood pressure looks a lot better than it did earlier. Detective, why don't you go get a cup of coffee or something? I need to check her stitches."

"Uh, okay. Rukhsana, I'll keep you posted if there's any news about your dad, or if we hear something from forensics. I'll swing by later to see if you want to add anything to my notes."

"Thank you, Detective. I appreciate it," she said. They watched him wrap his coat over his forearm and exit the hospital room with Officer West on his heels.

"Girl, I thought he was going to stay in here all night," Sheila said, chuckling.

"You and I both, Sheila."

"He's got it bad, doesn't he? You better watch out or he'll make you his wife."

"Please," Rukhsana said, pulling her hijab forward so that Sheila could untie the back of her gown. "I have no desire to be a cop's wife." *Or anyone else's, for that matter.* "My mother worried about my father my whole life. My dad says her anxiety became worse after they had me. I don't envy that at all."

"Your poor mother went through a lot. She probably worried because he was trying to run a police station and a mosque. That's two full-time jobs on top of being a family man. Looks like a few of your stitches have popped loose. I'll get one of the doctors to look at them in a bit."

"It's true," Rukhsana said. "But he was a part-time imam. He mostly dealt with spiritual counseling."

Sheila stopped fussing over Rukhsana's bandages. "You mean exorcisms, right?"

"That's right. My dad visited the homes of people who had spiritual ailments and helped them heal."

"Why'd he stop?" Sheila asked, cutting off a strip of medical tape. "Don't mind me, Rukhsana. People in this town talk and I'm just being nosy."

Rukhsana smiled and patted her friend on the hand. "It's not nosy, Sheila. I'm surprised you've never asked me or heard it from one of the other nurses. They used to love talking behind my back when I worked here. My father stopped performing exorcisms because he didn't like bringing his work home with him."

"Oh, Lord. You mean... spirits would follow him home?"

"Yes. He told my mother that he could see them near our house."

"I think I'm going to have nightmares too," Sheila said, shivering. "I don't know if I believe in all of that, but it freaks me out anyway."

Rukhsana smiled. "I'm sorry. I didn't mean to scare you."

"It's my own fault. I love hearing scary stories, but I always pay the price later," she said, taking off her gloves. "If your daddy gave up performing exorcisms because the spirits followed him home, I can't blame him for that, sis. I probably would have sold my house and left town."

"My mother convinced him to quit when she caught him teaching me how to perform them. Eventually, she saw them for herself and changed her mind. She wanted him to continue teaching me, but by then, he'd taken her advice to heart and considered the whole thing too dangerous for the family."

"He's pretty upset that you've followed in his footsteps, but I for one am eternally grateful."

Rukhsana and Nurse Randall turned towards the door. A slight woman with an olive complexion wearing a white lab coat stood there.

"As Salaamu Alaikum, Naureen," Rukhsana said.

"Wa Alaikum As Salaam, Rukhsana. How's she looking, Nurse Randall?"

"A couple of popped stitches, but all things considered, she's doing well, Doctor Ahmed," Nurse Randall said. "She's telling me scary stuff that's going to keep me looking over my shoulder all night. I'm sure I'll be wondering what's hiding under my bed when I get home, too," she said, smiling wide as she eased Rukhsana into the lumpy hospital pillows.

"Say an extra prayer, tonight," Doctor Ahmed said.

"Oh, you can count on it. I'll probably say dozens. Rukhsana, I'll send someone over as soon as I can. If your father shows signs of improvement, I'll let you know."

"Thanks, Sheila," Rukhsana said. Doctor Ahmed closed the door when the nurse left and approached the bed. "Is this a friendly visit or a professional one, Naureen?"

The tiny Arab woman put her hands on her hips and squared off. "Rukhsana, what are you and your father up to? Are you trying to open the gates of Hell or something?"

CHAPTER NINE

"WE AREN'T TRYING to open the gates of hell, Naureen. It was a routine exorcism gone wrong." Rukhsana sat up in the bed again, wincing. Her neighbor and close family friend, Doctor Naureen Ahmed, dropped the tote bag she carried and sat down in the chair next to the bed.

"You look really uncomfortable."

"It's not so bad now that the morphine is kicking in."

"From what I've heard, Rukhsana, it sounds to me like you and your daddy caused a lot of mayhem this evening. Two dead cops and two dead civilians? That must be a personal best."

"I can't believe they're gone. I knew all of them. Poor Laiba and Daniyal. He was just a kid, Naureen. And Pike and Marlon were good cops. My father trusted them, or he wouldn't have brought them along. I failed them all." She thought about the poor officers who laid their lives on the line in a fight for which they were ill prepared. Their blood was on her hands.

"Don't be so hard on yourself, Rukhsana. You and I both know these things are unpredictable. Sometimes, losing people is inevitable."

"Maybe it's time that I give this up."

"Now is the perfect time for you to be doing this. Hundreds of people would be lost right now if you hadn't intervened and fought against the evil inside them. I would be lost too."

Rukhsana glanced at Naureen. Neither of them could help thinking about Naureen's birthday party all those years ago. It was the last one either ever had, or attended.

The possession had splintered the lives of the Ahmed family. Two years after the party, Naureen was whisked away in the middle of the night to a home for troubled Muslim youth for safekeeping until she turned eighteen. Rukhsana and her parents took pity on the poor girl, visiting and nurturing her back to health. Eventually, with the help of her mother and father, Rukhsana unlocked the door hidden deep within her, releasing her from the jinni's prison.

"I heard that a woman is on the loose, and a wild dog too?"

"Would you believe me if I told you the wild dog is the woman?"

"Absolutely. After everything I've been exposed to in my life, how could I not? Why are you smiling like that?"

"Oh, I was just thanking Allah that I've got you on my side. Otherwise, I would start to question my sanity."

"Girl, please. I'm a medical professional; day after day I treat the mentally disturbed, and none of their stories comes close to the stuff you tell me."

"Great. I'm worse than the mentally disturbed," Rukhsana said, pressing the morphine drip boost. She knew it wasn't doing anything for her, but the placebo effect might help her brain believe that the pain would lessen anyway. Tricking yourself with a dummy button is true insanity.

"Hey, if you do go bonkers, I've got a nice calming room with fresh padded walls especially for you. The maintenance guys installed it last night so you won't have to bang your head into anyone else's sweat."

"Perfect timing. How did you know I was coming in?" The women laughed and a sharp pain passed down Rukhsana's spine. It hurt.

"Let's get you another blanket." Doctor Ahmed opened the tiny cabinet next to the bed and pulled out a small blue blanket, barely thicker than the sheets. "It's not much, but I can bring you one from home tomorrow."

"Don't bother. I'm signing out of here as soon as I can."

"I doubt they'll let you go that early. You look terrible."

"Doesn't matter. I can't be next to Abi as long as they have me tethered to this bed."

"What happened to him?"

"I'm not sure. Mariya, the one who escaped? She did something to him. I saw her put her mouth over his, like she was forcing him to take something in."

"Like what? Do you think the jinni tried to enter his body?"

"It's possible. But I don't think she succeeded. That's why she chose to run."

"Creepy."

"Yeah."

Naureen's pager went off and she rose to her feet. "Duty calls. See if you can get some sleep, okay? I'll check on you later."

"Okay. Thanks for coming by. Think you can sneak me into my dad's ward later?"

"I'll try. If nurse Hodge is working you can forget it."

"She's still here? I thought she retired."

"Still here and still a sour, bitter old woman."

"Tonight gets better and better, doesn't it?"

"Oh, before I forget, I've got some clothing for you and something else." Naureen picked up the tote bag and handed it to Rukhsana.

"What's this?" she asked, looking inside. Rukhsana pulled out a white parcel addressed in care of herself with Naureen's address on it. "Ah, it arrived."

"What is it?" Naureen asked.

"A patrilineal test kit from Kinect DNA."

"Are you still trying to convince your dad to take one of those? You know he's strong on his conspiracy theories. There's no way he's giving up a sample."

"He'll come around. I thought I had him the last time. He felt guilty when I said it would make me feel closer to him and mom now that she's passed."

"That's dirty, Rukhsana. Nice angle though, hitting him with guilt. You should have been a therapist."

"Why? Does guilt-tripping work for you?"

"Sometimes. But mostly no."

"Abi told me he'd think about it. I found it in the trash a few days later."

"Ouch. Here's a thought. You could get a sample from him while he's in his current state. I doubt he'd know."

Rukhsana frowned. "I can't do that to him, Naureen. It's illegal, not to mention unethical. They'd take your license for talking like that."

Naureen held up her hands. "Whoa, partner. I didn't say I would do it. I said you could do it and none would be the wiser."

"I'm not gonna do it. I'll just have to wait for Abi to come around."

"Suit yourself." Naureen checked her loud and incessant pager. "Gotta go. Get some sleep. And when you get out of here and get some rest, I'm gonna cook you a great big home-cooked meal."

"InshaAllah. Salaam," Rukhsana said. She settled into the bed and forced herself not to move. If she got any sleep at all tonight, it would be a miracle.

CHAPTER TEN

"I FEEL STIFF AS A BOARD," Rukhsana said, yawning into the back of her hand. She didn't expect to sleep, but at some point during the night, the rhythmic beeping of the machines monitoring her heart rate soothed her, just like it used to when she worked the late shift as an RN on these very floors.

The hospital had once been a second home to her, and last night it had given her a sense of respite to smell the cleaning solutions and iodoform, which everyone else called the 'hospital smell.' Most people associated the smell with death and disease, but she always thought it was the smell of hope and last resorts. After all, babies were born in hospitals and people were given second, sometimes third chances at life. She supposed it was all in how you looked at it.

She'd finally allowed her body to relax sinking into the hard mattress on her right side. Her shoulder had stiffened from not turning over during the night. When she slept that way, it was a clear sign of exhaustion.

"It's no wonder with all the stress you've endured." A new nurse, one named Lincoln, had taken over halfway through the night shift. "The doctor says you can leave in a couple of days," Nurse Lincoln said.

She was on until twelve, then a new face would pop up to read her chart, check her vitals and promise to come see her again in a little while. That visit would be followed up by the cleanup crew who came by to collect the food trays left over from the eleven o'clock lunch drop-off. In between the morphine naps and visits, Rukhsana would escape.

It would be easier to convince the new nurse to sign her out without hassle if Lincoln were busy trying to wrap things up and go home. She'd get her family doctor to administer pain medication later. After she got dressed, she planned to swing over to her father's room on the sixth floor. Naureen had come by in the early morning to catch her up on her father's condition but the news hadn't been what she hoped to hear.

"I'm sorry, love, there's no change. Your father is comfortable, but he's still exhibiting catatonia. It's probably due to emotional distress."

"Probably? Come on, Naureen, you know it is. I was so stupid, calling him out there like that. I knew he couldn't handle it, but they cornered me and I panicked. This is my fault."

"Nope. We are not going to start blaming ourselves for things that are out of our control," Naureen had said. "You know as well as I do that the both of you are stronger when you work together. I guess he got caught off guard and freaked out."

"I'll never forgive myself if he doesn't come out of this."

"Shh, Rukhsana, please. He'll be up and running in no time. I can feel it." Naureen had placed her arms around her and rocked back and forth until the tears stopped flowing and the sobbing spasms had subsided. Eventually, she lay down again and drifted off to sleep until Nurse Lincoln showed up.

"I know what you're thinking, Rukhsana," Nurse Lincoln said. "You're thinking, you'll run out of here during shift change and none will be the wiser, right?"

Rukhsana smiled. "What do you mean?"

"Don't play coy. All the nurses do it. None of them like to be on the other side of the hospital bed. It makes them feel helpless." The nurse smiled with a look of kindness in her eyes. "Look, I heard about your dad and I'm devastated. I can't imagine what you must be going through. All of us at the hospital absolutely adore the chief. We're all rooting for him."

"Thank you," Rukhsana said, holding back tears as she juggled talking and holding a digital thermometer in her mouth. Now that her body had rested and the adrenaline had worn off, her brain was sending her emotions into overdrive.

"I'll tell you what. If you agree to stay one more night and let us help you fight off the infection, I'll wheel you to your father's floor and you can spend as much time with him as you want. Do we have a deal?"

"What's my temperature?" Rukhsana asked.

"It's one oh one point five," the nurse replied, sliding the thermometer into its protective sleeve. "What do you say, Rukhsana? Can I count on you to let us do our jobs?"

Rukhsana sat back in the bed with a huff. "Sure."

"Alright, sweetie. I'll get someone to take you upstairs in a little bit. I promise."

"Thanks," Rukhsana said. Nurse Lincoln closed the curtain around the bed to give her privacy and left the room.

Rukhsana reached into the drawer next to the bed and pulled out her laptop. The good thing about having a close relationship with your neighbor is getting things from home when you can't get it yourself. Naureen used the spare key to get inside the house and grab some amenities, including her laptop and her favorite quilt that she'd sewn with her mother. Hours in the hospital room felt like years without entertainment. Maybe that's why she wanted to escape.

She opened her laptop and began sifting through her emails. There were six from Iman. Rukhsana had completely forgotten to contact her boss this morning to explain what happened. It looked like good news had traveled fast. The headline of the sixth email told her not to worry, that Iman was praying for her. Rukhsana scrolled down past the masjid announcements and spam until she saw something that made her sit up straighter.

Every time she saw the name, something about it made the hairs on the back of her neck stand up. Doctor Victor Reneau. They met online after she gave Kinect DNA permission to share her results with those in the database who were a match. She received a notification two days later in her inbox that there was one DNA match in the database. The match was a young Black man from Virginia in his early thirties. He was her first cousin.

Victor emailed her three days later, asking enough questions to film a three hour documentary about her life. She told him there must be some mistake. Neither of her parents had living relatives, nor did they have siblings. He told her that she was adopted and she set her account to private. There must have been some mistake.

Two months later, curiosity got the better of her and she made her account public again. Maybe Kinect had gotten their act together and found some real information about her real relatives, not this Victor character. Within an hour, Victor had sent over ten messages, pleading for her to answer.

Rukhsana figured anyone who was that insistent was either in need of Naureen's therapy or believed with all his heart that they were related. He got his wish. She felt sorry for him and dialed the phone number he had asked her to call. She used the last public pay phone in town, right outside the police station.

"Rukhsana, I can't believe you called," he said into the phone.

"Hello, Victor. If I hadn't called you, how would I get you to stop emailing me?" He'd laughed, his tone warm and full, and she knew right then that she liked him. She especially liked his rich accent. It wasn't like her Virginian accent, so she asked him about it.

"My mama was from New Orleans, but she lived here most of her life," he explained. "My twin brother Vincent and I picked it up from her, but my other siblings sound like my daddy did."

She quickly discovered that they could talk shop too. He was a doctor, an ophthalmologist, but he hadn't been practicing for a couple of years. "How come?" She asked.

"I was letting stress get to me."

"Long hours?"

"Let's say it's time to hang it up when the eye doctor is the one who's seeing things," he said.

"What do you mean? Were you having hallucinations?"

"No. It's hard to explain. I would examine my patients and feel like someone was looking back at me. Like a second pair of eyes."

"Someone besides the patient?" Rukhsana asked. There was a long pause on the other end of the phone. "Victor? Are you there?"

"I'm sorry, Rukhsana. I don't mean to sound odd."

"You don't," she said, nodding at the guys from the hardware store as they walked by. "It sounds like you're trying to tell me something without telling me something."

"I suppose I am," he said. He laughed again, but this time it sounded weaker, tinged with a touch of sadness. "How do I say this without scaring you off?"

"What is it? Are you ill? Do you need a kidney or something?"

"Are you religious?" He asked.

"You could say that," she said.

"Good. Do you believe in God and angels and... the devil? Do you believe the devil exists?"

"I do." The conversation had taken a turn that she hadn't anticipated. Her first worry had been that he wanted money or something else tangible. Not religious beliefs. Was he trying to convert her?

"Okay. Do you think a person can become influenced by him?"

"By the devil?"

"Yes. Do you, Rukhsana Davis, first cousin to Doctor Victor Renau, number one nutcase in Rosewood Hollow, Virginia, believe that a person can be influenced by the devil?"

"Victor, is this some kind of joke? Did my father put you up to this?"

"Your father? Brother Benjamin Davis?"

"Brother Benjamin Davis? So you do know him?"

"I only met him once. That was when he and Sister Clara came to the family church and took you away."

"What are you talking about Victor? I don't understand."

"Brother Benjamin and Sister Clara adopted you. Your real parents were killed and they agreed to keep you away from here."

"Keep me away from there? Why would they do that?"

"To protect you from the devil."

A chill ran through her. "Victor, what do you know about exorcisms?"

I know that it's going to take a lot more than a nice old man in a black suit with a white collar to defeat what plagues our family. Something is out there, Rukhsana, lying in wait. It's searching for us and taking us out one by one."

"Who are you talking about?" She asked.

"Family members. You're not the only one who was separated from the rest of us. There are others."

"I don't understand what you mean, Victor. Why would your family separate the children? And if it's true, where are they?"

"Close. The elders vowed that they'd never contact you, but I'm starting to wonder if you're in more danger now because you don't know who you are or where you come from."

Rukhsana looked down the street at the flux of traffic. A man stepped off the sidewalk into the oncoming traffic. Rukhsana's eyes jutted open as the cars passed right through him. The jinn, no longer content to bother her at home, made themselves known to her everywhere she went.

"Rukhsana, are you still there?"

"Yes, Victor, I'm here. This is a lot of information to take in. I don't know what to make of it. Adoption, the devil, lost children. It sounds..."

"Crazy," Victor said.

"Plausible," she said.

"What?"

"I said, it sounds plausible."

"I didn't expect that. I thought you'd tell me to take a hike."

"I can assure you, everything you're saying sounds pretty run of the mill for me in my line of work."

"You're a nurse, right?"

"I used to be."

"What do you do now?"

"I banish the second pair of eyes, Victor."

Rukhsana remembered the conversation like it was yesterday. She ordered another test, hoping to investigate Victor's claims further. Her father's refusal to take the DNA test only increased her curiosity.

Why was he so reluctant? It's not like he was a criminal trying to hide his identity from the authorities. When he recovered, she'd give it one more try and ask him to take the test. After that, she'd consider it a lost endeavor. For now, she had other things to worry about, like her father's health, and the email from Victor marked, "URGENT."

CHAPTER ELEVEN

"ARE you ready to visit your father, sweetheart?" A petite woman wearing a volunteer badge pushed open the door to Rukhsana's hospital room and brought in a wheelchair. "Nurse Lincoln said that you were anxious to see the chief. I told her I'd be glad to help you out." She brought the chair right up against the bed and started organizing the IV stand.

"I appreciate it. Thank you, Miss..."

"Benito," the woman said.

"Thank you, Miss Benito. I would love to see him." Rukhsana closed her laptop and put it away. The volunteer helped her into the awaiting chair, and they glided down the hallway to the elevators. She was anxious to read Victor's email, but it would have to wait until later. His communication had fizzled out over the past few weeks, and in the back of her mind, she worried about him. He told her that something was happening in Rosewood Hollow, something vague about one of their cousins. He hadn't given her a name, but his elusive behavior didn't go unnoticed.

The whole thing left her conflicted. Victor was a total stranger hailing from a place she'd never had a reason to visit. He'd entered her life, hellbent on convincing her that she was adopted. It was insane. But she found herself intrigued by the notion.

Growing up, her mother had been ambiguous about her roots. Her reluctance to talk about her life left Rukhsana asking questions on her deathbed days before she fell into a coma. Her mother hadn't been cooperative, even pretending not to hear. Either way, she died with her secrets intact. Rukhsana couldn't understand it.

Most people had extended family, or a logical explanation about why they didn't, but according to her mother, they didn't exist and didn't matter. Rukhsana would have felt better if she'd told her a lie. Why couldn't they be living in a condo in Dallas, or on an island in the Caribbean? Her mother had been honest to a fault, except about her family. If Victor was telling the truth, Rukhsana needed proof.

"Here we are, hon. Sixth floor," Miss Benito said, interrupting her train of thought. They exited the elevator and headed down a hall identical to the ones on her floor, minus the incessant traffic. The nurse's station sat empty, with a sign-in sheet sprawled across a small table for visitors.

The floor was too quiet. Besides the noises coming from machinery, she could hear Miss Benito breathing as she rolled her around a corner towards the back end of the ward. Rukhsana saw beautiful bouquets and balloons, a birthday party banner, get-well-soon cards. It depressed her that many of these patients would never see the gifts brought by their visitors. She selfishly muttered a plea, asking that her father wake up.

"Miss Benito, can I borrow you for a moment?" A tall blonde nurse stepped into the hallway.

"Sure. You don't mind, do you, Rukhsana? I'll be quick," Miss Benito said, locking the wheelchair brakes.

Before Rukhsana had a chance to reply, she found herself against the wall, facing the long corridor. Unable to move, she settled into the wheelchair and closed her eyes. Something about the familiar sounds and smells reminded her of her late-night shifts, long after visitor hours were over and the patients were asleep. The familiarity allowed her to relax until her chin rested on her chest.

A violent swipe across her cheek woke her with a start. Rukhsana's body jerked and the wheelchair hit the wall. Someone had pushed her towards the exit at the opposite end of the hall. Her hand wiped blood from her cheek where something sharp had dragged across her face. "Miss Benito?"

Rukhsana gripped both wheels and pushed, ignoring the pain shooting through her injured forearm and back. She bit down, grinding her teeth, turning the wheelchair back towards her father's room at the far end of the hall. The effort broke her out in beads of sweat, making her stitches burn and itch. She took a break next to the stairway door and opened it. "Hello? Is anybody there?"

From her vantage point, the stairway looked empty. She listened for footfalls going up or down but heard nothing. Backing out of the doorway, she entered the corridor, careful of her forearm. If Miss Benito saw the blood seeping through her bandages, she'd wheel her back to her room canceling her visit.

Rukhsana listened, separating the currents running through the overhead lights from the usual low-frequency sounds in the ICU. The stillness that relaxed her earlier now made her shudder. Where were the coughing patients and crying family members? Rukhsana urged the wheelchair forward until the pain became unbearable. She blotted the steady stream of blood from her cheek with the shoulder of her hospital gown. She needed help or she'd be stuck in the hallway forever. "Hello?"

The lights switched off, followed by the dying hum of electricity. Rukhsana took a deep breath and counted to three, expecting the backup generator to bring up the lights. Darkness had never triggered fear in her, but given the last twenty-four hours, the hairs on her arms stood at attention.

At the far end of the hall, a door opened. A figure dressed in dark clothing entered the corridor. In slow, deliberate movements, it turned to face her. Although she wore her glasses, Rukhsana squinted. "Hello? Have you seen any nurses? The generator's not working."

Whoever it was stood motionless, watching her. An odd sensation passed through her, and instinct told her one thing; stay away from the darkness. *The evil.* Rukhsana removed her glasses and saw vibrant blue and deep red shrouding the figure. She blinked and peered at it.

"Hello? Can anyone hear me?" With the last ounce of strength in her arms, Rukhsana wheeled to the nearest room on the left side and knocked on the door. All the doors on either side of the ward opened at once. Frigid, stale air poured into the ward.

She peered into the nearest room. The crisp white sheets had been replaced with black linens, the walls a dark nothingness that she could peer into forever. She looked to her right. The room was a mirror image of the last one. Rukhsana had never seen anything like this. Her experiences had never been so surreal as to experience a change in the environment. Was she hallucinating?

The unmistakable sound of cloven feet struck the floor. The figure had stepped towards her. She tracked it in the dark by the cast of its aura. The distance between them closed at an alarming rate; the entity had reached the halfway point between them in mere seconds.

"Audhubillah. May Allah forbid it." Rukhsana patted her side. She had left her Qur'an on the bedside table in her room. It made no difference; she'd memorized it anyway.

Rukhsana inhaled, sucking in air and releasing it until she was on the brink of hyperventilation. The wrenching pain of anxiety gripped her heart. Seasoned exorcist or not, fear was real. She gulped slow breaths until she found her nerve.

"In the name of Allah, I command you to leave this place." It paused, tilting its head, considering her. Rukhsana sat up in the chair, straightening her posture. The creature moved again at a slower pace. Rukhsana rubbed her hands together, massaging the icy sensation from her fingers.

A low, guttural sound vibrated in the walls and through the floor until she could feel it in her legs. It was closer. The stench of the creature filled her nasal cavity now.

Her eyes grew wide. The floor rumbled underneath her chair until she couldn't discern her thunderous heartbeat from the creature's charge. The frigid air crackled against the tremendous heat emerging from the jinni. Rukhsana's skin broke out in blisters the nearer it came. She'd run out of time. Her fingers gripped the arms of her chair as she braced for impact.

Rukhsana screamed as she watched the creature dive into her chest, searing the flesh between her breasts as it entered her. Her hands raised in a feeble attempt at warding it off. She felt herself sway and jerk as the beast transformed from flesh, hair, claws and hooves into pure fire. Her stomach distended, threatening to burst.

Blackness consumed her disorientated mind and Rukhsana doubled over, face into lap. She saw herself killing innocent people. Traveling great distances across space and time. Corrupting souls. The more she gave in to the impulse to let the entity take over, the less she felt pain. Her mind relaxed, allowing itself to take a back seat to someone else's thoughts and actions. Then she remembered something her mother once said. *Pain is good. Discomfort is life.*

Right now, she didn't believe it, didn't see how that could be true. 'Your mother is a liar!' the entity told her. Aren't we all? Rukhsana thought. Still. How bad could it be, letting the entity control her? She could stay hidden in the darkness and never be haunted by another jinni, never need to perform another exorcism. Someone else could do it. But who? And what would become of Abi?

She sat up in the chair and coughed. The act burned the back of her throat, but she did it again. She coughed once more, increasing the intensity. Her swollen belly rumbled and she took a deep breath, exhaling from deep within her diaphragm until she felt heat travel up her throat. Rukhsana kept at it, huffing and panting like a woman in labor. Inch by inch, the creature lost traction and began traveling upwards in her esophagus. She felt more like herself and began aggressively breathing out the demon until her mouth tasted of bile. Almost there. Once she felt the weight of it sitting on her chest, she shoved three fingers down her throat. The contents of her stomach emptied, along with a mass of hair, feathers, and bone.

"Audhubillah." The remains of the creature burst into flame. The lights turned on and an ear-splitting screech tore Rukhsana's attention away from the smoldering remains.

This time, she didn't hesitate. Her hands clung to the wheels forcing her body to cooperate. High on a fresh supply of adrenaline, she swung the chair around in a near-cataclysmic crash with the wall and wheeled herself to the fire ax box mounted on the wall. *In Case of Emergency.* Damned right it was.

"Roxie, whoa, whoa!"

Rukhsana withered under the vice-like grip around her wrist. Slight pressure on her shoulder sent her into flight or fight mode. She wrenched her wrist free from the hold and shot an elbow into the soft middle of her assailant. A hand slapped her hard across the face.

"Naureen?" Rukhsana rubbed her face. "You slapped me?"

"Yes, I slapped you. What the hell is wrong with you? Are you trying to trigger the alarm?"

"Naureen, something attacked me. See my face?"

"There's nothing on your face except where I knocked some sense into you."

Rukhsana rubbed the spot where the injury from the jinni had been. "Naureen, I was in the hallway waiting for Miss Benito."

"Who?"

"Miss Benito. She's a volunteer."

"If you say so."

She looked at her friend sideways. "How do you think I got up here?"

Naureen shrugged. "Elevator. Anyway, Miss Benito..."

"Right. While I waited for her, the power went out—

"The power?" Naureen looked up at the lights.

"Yes. And a jinni attacked me. Naureen, it was inside of me."

"Are you saying you're possessed?"

"No, I am not possessed."

Naureen clicked her pen and reached into her pocket. "When's the last time you got some sleep?"

"Last night. What are you doing?"

"Writing you a prescription."

"For what?"

"For peace of mind."

"No thanks. I want to remain clear-headed. Something's going on and I need my wits about me if I'm going to figure it out."

"You know, I can't see you on a professional level, Roxie, but I can recommend someone I trust."

"Fuck off, Naureen. You know that I'm not crazy." Rukhsana grabbed the wheels and backed the wheelchair into the wall until it got stuck in the corner.

"Damn, sis, no need for hostility. I'm the last person to call you crazy," she said, helping Rukhsana with the chair. She got behind her and pushed her down the hall towards her father's room. "All I'm saying is that the power didn't go out, Roxie. You're carrying a heavy load that would make anyone stressed. There's nothing wrong with making sure you keep your sanity."

"Do you believe me or not?"

Naureen stopped the wheelchair and crouched before her friend. "I believe you."

Rukhsana exhaled. She needed Naureen to believe her. After all, hadn't the roles been switched all those years ago? "Thanks. Sorry I swore at you."

"I'm used to it. Occupational hazard."

"Then I feel even worse for doing it."

"Good. Let's go see your dad."

NAUREEN WHEELED Rukhsana to the last door on the hall and opened it wide enough for them to pass through. "Here we are. He's got the best room on the ward. Salaam, Chief, I've got a surprise for you. Your daughter's here. Shit, he's still out," Naureen said, rolling the chair near the bed. "Hey, I'm gonna give you two some time alone. Let me know if you decide to go home."

"I will. Thanks for putting me in check out there."

"That's what friends are for." Naureen backed out of the room and closed the door.

Rukhsana reached over and untucked the covers. His hand fell into hers, hot and clammy. You never knew what you were going to get in these rooms. Freezing cold or boiling. She let go and pulled a wad of tissues free from a box on the table, dabbing at the beads of sweat on his forehead, then tossed the tissues into the garbage and took his hand again.

"As Salaamu Alaikum, Abi. It's me, Rukhsana. Don't mind my hands, it's cold on the third floor." Her father lay in the bed, still as the rest of the ward. She began massaging his palm with her thumb and forefinger, hoping to elicit a response.

Her father lay there, staring at the ceiling. "I caused a big mess this time, Abi. I'm sorry that I went behind your back to perform ruqya. Detective Wright is on the case as usual. He thinks I'm delusional. I swore to Allah that I was done with it, but something keeps sucking me back in." She let go of her father's hand and checked her face in the bedside mirror. "This thing that I do is important, but it's not worth more than your life. I hope to Allah that I can fix things." She ran her fingers along four flesh-colored slash marks that appeared on her cheek. On a hunch, she pulled back her hijab and hospital gown. There was a two-inch scar in the area between her breasts.

Chapter Twelve

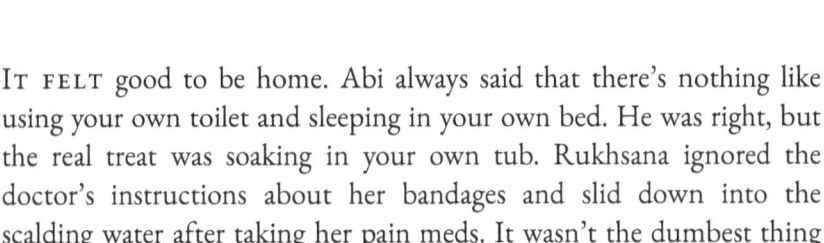

It felt good to be home. Abi always said that there's nothing like using your own toilet and sleeping in your own bed. He was right, but the real treat was soaking in your own tub. Rukhsana ignored the doctor's instructions about her bandages and slid down into the scalding water after taking her pain meds. It wasn't the dumbest thing she'd ever done, taking a bath after popping a few narcotics, but it was up there. Some people drank wine; she took hot baths.

She thought of Naureen and how the once troubled teen had grown into a self-assured doctor. These days, Naureen was just as quick to explain away odd occurrences with science rather than acknowledge the possibility of an otherworldly explanation. She stayed ready, a prescription pad burning a hole in her pocket. Unless Rukhsana reminded her. Science couldn't explain everything. It's not that she wanted her friend to dwell in her hellish past, or discount the importance of science; she wanted Naureen not to forget faith as a powerful component to healing.

Most people didn't believe in a higher power anymore. They were spiritual until they met actual spirits. Then, they were scared.

Gifted by an ignorant, but well-meaning aunt, it had been a talisman that attracted unwanted attention all those years ago.

Rukhsana had found the tiny bag containing rolled up pieces of paper inked with mysterious symbols and numbers. *Taweez.* Meant to ward off evil, the amulet invited the jinni to enter her friend.

The constant drip from the sink's faucet shifted Rukhsana's thoughts to her father. His life consisted of law enforcement and half-finished home improvements. He never quite got to tinkering with the plumbing. She'd have to do it herself if she wanted peace. But not now. The hot water called her name and she answered by sliding deeper into the tub, careful not to wet the fresh bandages on her forearm or her cornrows. The last thing she wanted to do was wash her hair.

Unable to fight it, she drifted off.

The lone drip had turned into several. Drip, drip, drip. Tap. Rukhsana squeezed her already closed eyes. Drip, drip, drip. SPLAT. Droplets hit her square in the forehead. She craned her neck and looked up at the ceiling.

Sticky red ooze dripped from her body into the bathtub. Her hand flew over her mouth. Rukhsana sat up and swallowed the bile that crept up her throat. When she pulled her hand away from her mouth, she found the bandage on her forearm soaked through and coated in dark viscous blood, as was her hair and body. She'd been bathing in blood.

The walls had been coated in their entirety. It was everywhere. The sink. The floor. Lightbulbs. It was as though she saw the world through red contact lenses.

Thick globs slipped through her fingers and toes like weeds embedded in the lake where Abi took her fishing. With great effort, she stood and shook the muck from her limbs, sloughing off the dried bits.

Her feet splashed on the soggy bath mat as she exited the tub, spattering her already grime-coated legs. The room closed in around her as the knots in her stomach multiplied. If she could make it into the hall, she'd be alright. The doorknob slipped between her fingers.

"Ya Allah." She gripped the knob with both hands, jerking and twisting it. Rukhsana let go and snatched a blood-soaked hand towel from the rack, wiping her sticky fingers with it. *What's the point?* She tossed it aside on the soiled countertop.

What was the point of anything if she didn't get her act together?

Now was the time to gain back control or admit defeat and fall into darkness. She picked up her bloody bath towel and wrapped it around her naked body.

"Is this the best you can do?" She smacked the door with open palms in a show of bravado, followed by immediate regret. The shock of pain traveled up her injured arm and down the criss-cross slashes on her back in waves. "Yeah, I'm hurt, but not like you're gonna be," she said, hitting the door again out of sheer defiance.

Behind her, the squeak of stainless steel shower curtain hooks dragged along the double rod. In achingly slow motion, she watched from the mirror as the curtain closed.

BLOOD AND SILENCE. Hairs standing on the back of her neck, Rukhsana stood in front of the mirror at an angle, watching the shadow behind the curtain watch her. Never had her experience with the super-natural been so extreme. They were showing themselves without fear. If the barrage continued much longer, there would be serious deleterious effects on her mental stability. She'd crack, like one of Naureen's patients who were beyond the scope of her care. They ended up in Ward D at Dominion Springs in Rosewood Hollow.

No. She was not gonna crack and she was not gonna lose this battle. She pivoted until she was within one foot of the curtain and raised her hand. Now or never. She reached for it, chickened out and ran back to the door. There were some things she didn't want to confront in the nude. She had to get out.

Her mind had told her that the room was full, that it couldn't hold any more blood. That was a lie. The walls could weep, the leaky faucet could hemorrhage, the nightlight could fill and burst, and then all the damned lights could go out. Again. Rukhsana banged on the door until the hinges rattled in the door frame. She would beat it down with her bare hands if she had to.

"Let me out, let me out!" Rukhsana tugged until she thought her arms would fall off, but the door held fast. Tears, salt and blood blinded her. The curtain pulled back. It was coming because she refused to fight it. To hell with that. The fight could carry on some other time. "LET ME OUT!"

The door flew open and Rukhsana landed flat on her ass, bathed not in blood, but light. She raised her hand, shielding her vision and her face from whatever being loomed over her.

"Okay, Rukhsana, you don't have to lose your shit. How many times has your daddy told you to jiggle the doorknob to the left then yank it to the right when the door sticks? What's wrong? Why are you crying? Are you hurt?"

"N-Naureen?" Rukhsana backed away until she hit the far wall.

"Of course, silly. Who else would it be? Do you want some help?"

"There's someone... I was taking a bath..."

"Why are you whispering?"

Rukhsana used her finger, filling the gaps where words failed her.

"The tub? Why were you in the tub anyway? You're supposed to take a sponge bath." Naureen yanked the curtain all the way open and peered into the bathtub. "Gross. There's blood all over the bath pillow. Gonna have to throw that away. You getting up off the floor or nah?" She offered a hand.

Rukhsana took it and pulled until she winced and yanked herself off the clean bath mat. "The lights went out," she offered as an explanation.

Naureen flicked the switch. "You turned them off?"

Dumbfounded, Rukhsana shook her head. "There was blood. In the tub."

"Uh huh, I see it. It's from your back. And your arm. What were you thinking?"

"It was full of blood, Naureen. The entire bathroom. I-I tried to get out and something was behind me in the tub."

"There's nobody here but us."

"Look at me. I'm covered in blood. It's all over me. It's on my arms and legs, it's in my hair."

"Rukhsana, let's take a deep breath and think this over. You were attacked yesterday. You're heavily medicated, you have extensive injuries, and have popped your stitches open. The blood is yours. And there's nobody else in the house. Are you seeing people? Do you hear them too?"

"Uh-uh, don't you start psychoanalyzing me, Naureen. I'm going through crazy shit, but I'm not crazy."

Naureen's nostrils flared. "There you go using that word again. Nobody called you that, so chill." She bent down and let the water out of the tub, then turned Rukhsana around and undid her cornrows. "Now, get in the shower, and wash off all that blood. I'll help you with your bandages and redo your hair when you get out."

"Will you stay with me?"

Naureen sighed and turned around. "Hurry up."

"THERE'S no sign of forced entry and I checked with your neighbors. No one saw anything strange, and since Naureen found the spare key under the mat, I don't think you should worry. Thanks." Detective Wright sat down at the kitchen table with a pen and paper and sipped the mug of coffee that Naureen passed to him.

"You're welcome. I told her there was nothing to worry about, but if it helps her sleep then I'm glad you came," Naureen said.

"You didn't have to come, Detective. I'm alright now." Rukhsana downed a mug of piping hot mint tea that Naureen brought from her trip to Oman last fall. On other occasions, they would make a big production of drinking it, passing it back and forth in glass tea cups to cool it, but not tonight. Tonight she needed the heat to scald the back of her throat, reminding her that she was alive and in the real world. It was the one thing she could count on. Pain.

"What was it that set you off?" he asked.

"I fell asleep in the bathtub then got locked in the bathroom. I guess the pain medication is making me a little loopy," Rukhsana said. He looked at her the way he always did, with a reassuring nod and eyes that said he didn't believe her. She hated it.

The first time she'd seen that expression was when he asked why she was waiting so long to get married. Her excuse had been that she wanted to pursue her career. When he asked again, she used her mother as an excuse. The third time her father's grief had been mentioned and she had hoped it was enough to keep him from asking a fourth.

The truth was, she would never marry. Not because she feared putting her husband in jeopardy, or because he wouldn't understand her need to serve the community with her gift. The truth was, she didn't want to. Not him, or anyone else.

She was content to come home and cook if she wanted to, or eat an entire box of crackers and canned processed cheese for dinner. She liked doing her own laundry, and coming and going as she pleased. As for natural urges, she never had them. After years of blood tests, therapy, (that Naureen didn't know about), and soul searching, she discovered and accepted that she was a content lone wolf.

"Is it normal for you to use the spare key?" he asked Naureen.

"No, but I didn't want to disturb her if she was sleeping. She's under a lot of stress."

Detective Wright scribbled something in his notepad. The women exchanged glances. "I placed a uniformed officer outside your father's room tonight," he said.

Rukhsana sat up. "Why?"

"Did something happen?" Naureen asked.

"Yes and no."

"Tell us," they said in unison.

"Hold on, don't get upset. Nothing happened to him, but a patient four doors down was attacked."

"By who?" Rukhsana dreaded the answer.

"Don't know. The patient was beaten and succumbed to his injuries before we could get an answer."

"When did this happen?" Naureen picked up her phone and scrolled through her missed messages.

"About three hours ago. We're running the security tapes for the hallway and staircases. As of now, the ICU is a crime scene so there will be no visitation for the next day unless the visitor is on the list. I placed your name on there, so you can still see your father whenever you feel up to it. For now, I suggest you take it easy for a day or two." Detective Wright stood.

"You're leaving?" Rukhsana put down her mug.

"Don't get up, Rukhsana. I can see my way out."

"Take care of yourselves ladies." The detective slid his chair under the table. "By the way, Rukhsana, if you have some time later in the week, I need to speak with you privately."

There it was. "About what?"

"Just some information the chief would want you to have. In case his condition continues for an extended period," he said.

"Oh." Rukhsana hadn't considered her father's fate yet. Everything had happened so fast. But it was premature to make plans like this. Her father could snap out of his state at any moment. "Alright Detective, call me later in the week when you have time."

He nodded and left the house.

"He's right. You should be thinking about the future," Naureen said. "Especially now that you won't have your father to help you."

"I get it."

"Do you?"

"Yeah. Stop talking to me like a child. Did you forget that I'm a grown woman? I'm capable of thinking for myself, you know." Rukhsana went to the sink and tossed out the rest of her tea. There were tiny slivers of glass in the sink leftover from the previous encounter in the kitchen.

"It sounds to me like you think I've crossed a boundary," Naureen said. "I respect that, and I apologize for sounding condescending. I'm concerned for you. I see you exhibiting signs of paranoia and possible hallucinations—

"I know what I saw."

"Let me finish, please. I see that you're distressed, and you believe that you're seeing things that I can't corroborate. It reminds me of your mother."

"Get out. I don't want to talk about my mother," Rukhsana said, pulling Naureen by the arm.

"Roxie, chill." Naureen rose from the table. "I'm your friend. I care about you."

"Like you were when my mother got hurt? I said go."

"That's unfair, Rukhsana. Your mother had a psychotic break." Naureen stepped into the entryway and put on her shoes.

"I wouldn't call an ambush by a vengeful jinni psychotic. What? What is that look?"

"It's nothing," Naureen said.

Rukhsana's eyes narrowed. "You didn't believe her, and you don't believe me, do you?" She waited for an answer.

Naureen sighed. "Goodnight, sis." She stepped out into the chilly night air and closed the door.

CHAPTER THIRTEEN

"I'VE BEEN TRYING to get you on the phone for days, Victor. Where have you been?"

Rukhsana waited in her father's hospital room for the doctor. Getting into the ICU had been more difficult than she'd imagined. Some time during the early hours, another patient had been beaten and killed.

Detective Wright had left implicit instructions for the uniformed officers, and still it had taken a personal phone call from him to convince them to budge. That left her in a sour mood, adding to the anxiety she already felt.

The fact that someone had murdered a patient put her on edge. She wondered if it made her selfish to hope that it had been a targeted individual and not a disturbed person on the loose. An unhinged killer made things uncertain. They could return at a moment's notice, leaving her father even more vulnerable to danger.

"Cousin, I apologize for leaving you in the lurch. Things got intense over here. Rosewood Hollow has a killer on the loose. One that requires my expertise, if you can believe it."

"The police need help with ophthalmology?"

"Floriography."

"What?" She racked her brain.

"In basic terms, I decipher the meaning behind flowers. Red roses means, love. Yellow roses, friend-zone."

"Gotcha. And that's an area of your expertise?"

"I have many hobbies, most I've acquired through necessity."

"So the killer is leaving flowers?"

"Black tulips."

"What do they represent?"

"I'm not supposed to discuss it."

"Oh."

"But I may need to break the rules this one time."

"How come?"

"Because I have a feeling this is personal. The first victim was a friend of mine. Well, she was more than that. Laura was family, though she didn't know it."

"I'm sorry for your loss, Victor."

"Our loss, Rukhsana. Laura was family, but she didn't know it."

Another long lost cousin? "Victor, why are there so many displaced people in your family?"

"Our family," Victor said. Rukhsana didn't respond. She knew what was coming next. Victor didn't like beating around the bush. "Did your father take the DNA test?"

"Not yet. Something's come up."

"It can't be more important than this."

"Wanna bet?" She glanced at her father. He hadn't stirred once in the hour that she'd been sitting with him. Even if he were to awaken, the last thing on her mind was questioning his parentage.

"You're doing something more important than saving lives?"

"Saving souls is more important."

"That doesn't sound like something a nurse would say."

"You're talking to the exorcist now."

"I don't know what that means, but it's imperative that you get your father to take that test. I think it's the only way you'll believe what I have to say."

"My father is unavailable for the unforeseeable future."

"He can't take a moment to spit into a tube?"

"No, he can't. To be honest, I don't know if I want to be a part of your family drama."

Victor kept silent. She opened her mouth to ask if he was still there; she heard him breathing and decided to wait.

"Rukhsana, I believe someone is trying to kill members of our family. I have a hunch about who it is, but I don't have definitive proof, or a reason why."

"You're working with the police. Why don't you tell them?"

"Because I think they might be involved." A knock on the door brought her back to reality.

"Victor, I'm sorry, but I need to end the call."

"You're serious? I dropped a bomb on you about our family and you have to end the call?"

"Sorry," she said. "This is a matter of life and death. You may be right about my parents, but that doesn't stop me from loving them. Goodbye." Rukhsana hung up the phone and waved Doctor Coleman into the room.

"Hello, Rukhsana, how are you holding up?" He lifted his pale white hand, splotchy with liver spots, and ran his fingers through his stark white hair. Rukhsana had known him for years, but noticed the older man's pale face had a yellow pallor and sagged. He'd been experiencing problems of his own, and she wondered how he found the strength to stay on his feet these days.

"As well as can be expected under the circumstances," Rukhsana said, rising from her chair. She hated being on this side of the transaction. She was supposed to give the bad news, not agonize over receiving it. Her father's chart still read the same. No changes to vital signs, no indication of the cause, and all that they could do was wait.

"Rukhsana, I've been over your father's charts and we've run every test there is. Frankly, I have no idea what's causing his coma. All we can do is wait and see."

She nodded. "Thank you, doctor."

"I know it's not what you want to hear."

Rukhsana held up her hands. "I get it. You're a good doctor. I know you're doing what you can for him. Listen, I've heard that there were murders on the floor? What's being done to make sure my father is safe?"

"You should be asking me that question." Detective Wright walked into the room and placed his hat on the table next to Chief Davis' bed.

"Back so soon, Detective?" the doctor asked.

"I can't sleep knowing the chief is here. The whole station is lost without him."

"They have you to rely on in the meantime," Rukhsana said.

"I do what I can, but I'm not him."

"Don't be modest, D'Angelo. I know what you do for my dad at the station. He has always appreciated you."

"Thank you for saying that, it means a lot," Detective Wright said. "So, is there any change, doc?"

"I was telling Rukhsana that there hasn't been a sign in one direction or the other. We're not sure what the issue is, but we're doing everything we can to get the chief back on his feet. It's important that you keep talking to him. He can hear us," Dr. Coleman said.

"Are you sure?" Detective Wright asked.

"Yes. He can hear voices and understand them. Of that, I'm absolutely positive. And don't wear yourselves out worrying about him. He needs you to take care of yourselves or there'll be hell to pay when he comes out of it."

"Don't I know it," Rukhsana said, nodding. Her father would fuss from morning to night if he thought they were losing sleep over him. He was the kind of man who liked to be the caregiver, not the other way around.

"Listen, I've got to make my rounds. If you need anything or you see a change, get the nurses to page me ASAP."

"You've got it, doctor. And thank you for taking care of him," Rukhsana said.

"Yeah, thanks, doc," Detective Wright said, closing the door after the doctor stepped out. He came back and sat down in an empty chair by the bed. "Have you been here long?"

"All morning. I need to get back to work or Iman is going to put a sign in the window looking for a replacement."

"She wouldn't do that. You're an asset to her store. She was losing business before you got there."

"I'm not an asset if I never show up."

"Don't rush, Rukhsana. You have injuries."

"I've been cleared to return to work."

"The chief wouldn't like you walking around with injuries."

"The chief doesn't pay my bills," she said, smiling.

Detective Wright smiled back. He leaned forward, looking like he wanted to tell her something but held back. She wasn't going to pry it out of him. He had his reasons for not telling her what was on his mind. If it were important, she was sure that he'd confide in her.

"Any leads on the suspect?" she asked, breaking the silence.

"Not yet. I plan to stay here tonight and watch over your father. I hope there's no more trouble, but if anyone comes onto the ward, I'll be here waiting for them."

"Please, be careful. The whole thing makes me sick to my stomach. Why would someone come onto the ward to kill people who are ill and suffering?"

He shrugged. "There could be a lot of reasons. I speculate that there's a logical explanation, one we haven't accounted for. The two patients had nothing in common, so I don't believe it was a hit. Still, there has to be something tying them together. We'll know more when we've thoroughly reviewed the surveillance tapes from the hallway."

"No one has reviewed them yet?"

"No. The head of security has been out sick, and he's the one with access to the tapes. I believe he'll be back tomorrow. In the meantime, I want you to go home and get some sleep. If you're returning to work, you at least deserve a good night's rest."

"Why are you leaning towards my father when you say that? Are you trying to win cool points?"

Detective Wright flashed her his perfect set of teeth. "Hey, the doctor said that he could hear us. At least he knows I'm looking out for his little girl."

"Tell him his little girl is just fine and there's no need to worry."

"I will. And I'll tell him that if she needs anything, day or night, all she has to do is call and I'll be there." His face transitioned from playful to serious. "I mean it, Rukhsana. Anything at all. Day or night."

"Thanks." She picked up her bag, gathering her things as she went around the room. "It sounds like Dad is gonna be in good hands here, so I'm heading home."

"Okay. I'll keep you posted if anything changes. Goodnight, Rukhsana."

"Goodnight D'Angelo." Rukhsana stepped out of the room and walked towards the exit at the other end of the hallway. An overwhelming unease settled in the pit of her stomach as she passed strips of yellow police tape cordoning off the rooms where patients had been attacked only a few hours before.

She considered asking Dr. Coleman if he would transfer her father to another hospital, but she knew that the staff would be offended if she suggested they weren't doing everything in their power to protect him. Then again, she didn't care what they thought; her father's safety mattered more than their feelings. Besides, it would come out of her pocket, and covering the ambulatory costs to move to a better hospital would be astronomical. And she knew that Detective Wright would take a bullet for her dad if he had to. It was how he'd gotten his rank in the first place.

There'd been a robbery at the grocery store on Main Street and her father had responded with Deputy Wright, at the time. They arrived as the two suspects were making a run for it. To the surprise of both parties, they'd met at the front door and shot it out. D'Angelo saw the first shot coming straight for the chief and jumped in the way, taking it in the shoulder. Rukhsana had been working at the hospital when they brought him in. The scar from the bullet wound looked like the old smallpox vaccine scars that her mother and father had on their arms. For now, she'd ride it out and let D'Angelo do his job.

She made it out to the parking lot and climbed into her car. The last place she wanted to go was home. But there was no other option unless she stalled and bought food for which she had no appetite. She could go to Naureen's, but it felt like the devil was trying his hardest to drive a wedge between them.

You're either a raaqi or you're not. Stop this foolishness, and go home. She reached into her pocket and rubbed the cover of her Quran between her thumb and forefinger. The paper cover had become smooth here, almost like goat-skinned leather. Her courage settled, and she drove home. From her vantage point, she couldn't see the dark figure snarling at her on the hospital's roof.

CHAPTER FOURTEEN

THREE HOURS into his voluntary shift at the bedside of Chief Davis, Detective D'Angelo Wright had grown bored of streaming movies. They were never the same when he watched them outside the comfort of his home. After a hard day at work, he liked to kick back with all the junk food he could handle while the fireplace roared in the background. The only thing missing was the woman of his dreams.

Most people might assume he was speaking in hyperbole when he called Rukhsana his dream woman, but he meant it. She checked off all the boxes for him. She was beautiful, educated, and from a good family. He didn't view her religion as a flaw; it was an obstacle, but one he was willing to work around.

Back in the day, when her mother was alive, he'd visited her at her firm and asked for Rukhsana's hand. She seemed put off by the suggestion that he pursue her daughter, but she made it clear that it wasn't because she thought him unsuitable for her. Over the course of the next year, he kept asking and her mother seemed to soften.

One day out of the blue, she'd let it slip that she got troublesome news from back home about a relative who was experiencing what she called, "spiritual warfare," and that none of them were as safe as her cousins had promised.

"Since when do you have relatives, Clara? Rukhsana told me that you and your husband didn't have any family."

"We messed up, D'Angelo. I hope one day she understands what we tried to do for her," she had said. He watched her eyes focus on something over his shoulder and turned to see at what she'd been staring, but there was nothing behind him but a painting with a field of black tulips.

"Is this new art?" he'd asked. "Looks kinda spooky." After that day, he watched an astute, professional woman come undone. She stopped coming to the office on time, and called in sick beyond the acceptable limit. When the firm had run out of warnings, she had been placed on indefinite leave. The night she came to clear out her office, the roof caved in, crushing her beneath it. Witnesses say they saw a woman in a red dress enter, but the rescue squad found no other survivors, nor did they recover a second body.

Days after the funeral, he received a mysterious package in the mail. The address had been scrawled in her hand. He'd opened it, curious as to what was inside, and found himself with more questions than answers. His first instinct had been to turn its contents over to the chief or Rukhsana, but his law enforcement training had sent him digging.

He put a lot of miles on his car, traveling back and forth between Salem and Rosewood Hollow, corroborating pages in the thick tome Clara had left. Tri-Cities Park held a lot of answers, one being what the mysterious black tulip looked like. The flower seemed anything but natural. It smelled like death, and felt like it too. He'd given his skin a vigorous scrub for the entire weekend to release the stench from touching one. He couldn't imagine how foul his hands would smell had he picked it and held it. And still, there were more questions.

When the questions led down a family tree that had been cleverly erased from most vital records, save for a few people, like a Doctor Vincent Renau and a few others, D'Angelo had headed to the Rosewood Hollow Genealogical Society and found another Reneau. Marcus. D'Angelo confronted the big man with busted boxer's knuckles and he had played dumb, even when D'Angelo mentioned Clara. But the face and hands never lied. Marcus had pulled his nose and opened his eyes wide every time he'd said something false, like an unfaithful spouse lying to his wife.

He let the questioning go after some time, but found himself being hounded by a nosy detective named Hanzlik. What the squat man had to do with the information Clara had given him was anyone's guess. After several weeks, the man stopped coming around, and D'Angelo busied himself with convincing Rukhsana via her best friend, Naureen, to take a DNA test.

He told Naureen to play along so that Rukhsana wouldn't know that it had been his idea. That turned out to be a mistake. Naureen had a sudden, feverish interest in why he wanted Rukhsana to take the test, and he'd had to pretend that he had an obsession with tracing people's roots back to their countries of ancestry. He'd even gotten one done and hung it up in his cubicle at work. The whole ordeal had been forgotten when the woman attacked the chief. It was a mystery that he'd unfold another time.

For now, he needed snacks. The chief lay in a coma as he had every night without so much as a peep. D'Angelo's stomach and boredom urged him out of his chair. There were plenty of deputies assigned to the hospital, but a look around wouldn't hurt, and the men would get a morale boost if he showed his face.

The detective shut off his phone and stepped into the hall. The quiet ambience of the critically ill and injured seemed more pronounced tonight. D'Angelo didn't like it.

He trained his eye on anything that looked out of place, scanning the bland artwork on the walls, the gentle reminders to turn off cell-phone ringers and sign in at the nurse's station. His shoes squeaked on the vinyl flooring as he moved towards the family room, prompting him to lighten his steps. He noted one man contorting himself into a painful position to accommodate the limited space on a loveseat, which D'Angelo guessed came off a factory floor twenty years ago.

D'Angelo stared with longing at the vending machines next to the sofa. It didn't seem right to wake someone sleeping in the ICU. He backed out of the room and continued his walk. The eerie beeping from the medical equipment reminded him of the time he'd been shot. His injury hadn't put him on this floor, but the amount of blood that poured from his wounds had materialized images of death that he hadn't been able to shake.

Death could happen at any time for anyone; he knew that. But the probability increased forty times in his line of work. He wished people knew that about cops. At the same time, he knew that possessing a firearm shaved off a large portion of private citizen's empathies.

When he reached the nurse's station, he nodded at the woman sitting behind the computer, typing. She nodded back and continued her work. Unlike nurses from the other floors, he'd never seen them talking and trading gossip. It was a no-nonsense ward, placing emphasis on patient comfort, at the risk of the nurses seeming cold and impersonal. He assumed they were under tremendous strain, handling distressed hysterical family members. Several times a week, they cared for transfers from the county jail clinic—patients most people would prefer not to see survive.

Past the station, the air grew cold, and he regretted leaving his uniform jacket in the chief's room. The overhead lights flickered between pale yellow and blue before settling on a sickly shade of green. He'd have to get one of the orderlies to replace the bulbs. He didn't want anything interfering with the security tapes or the deputies' ability to see in case something happened. When he reached the second family lounge at the opposite end of the floor, he found it empty.

D'Angelo fished out his wallet and used his debit card to load up on snacks. Next to the dentist, he found that hospitals had the tastiest, nutritionally void snacks. A core memory unlocked as he grabbed three bags of chips and four candy bars from the belly of the machine. He'd been in his teens then. He could still picture his father buying cigarettes from a vending machine that stood next to the sandwich fridge. His mother lay rotting from lung cancer in a bed down the hall. It had one of those pull levers that yanked the pack from its perch. When he was a kid, his mom used to let him pull the lever; he'd pretend he was in Vegas, sitting at a slot machine.

He grabbed a couple of root beers from the drink machine and stuffed them into his front pockets. It looked ridiculous, but he doubted anyone would care. The families who came to this floor rarely walked the halls anyway. He turned and dropped his snacks, startled by a woman standing behind him.

"Sorry, I didn't see you," he said, bending and picking up the plastic-wrapped junk. "Gotta get through the night," he said, standing. It looked like she'd had the honey-blonde lace-front wig she wore for a long time and had given up on untangling the matted ends. Her rail-thin collar and rib bones protruded from the tight blue shirt she wore.

D'Angelo searched her dark skin for open sores and discolorations indicating intravenous drug use. The strange green lighting made it difficult to discern if she had any track marks on her neck, and she suspiciously pulled her hands behind her back before he could get a better look. He tried a different approach.

"Are you visiting family? The nurses have asked everyone to sign in at the desk and receive a visitor's badge. I noticed yours is missing..."

The woman didn't respond. She remained planted between him and the doorway. Frustrated, he shifted all his snacks to his left hand and used the right one to gesture at the door. "I'm heading that way now. I can assist you in retrieving your badge, or maybe you left it in one of the rooms? I did the same thing with my jacket, and now I'm freezing," he said, forcing a chuckle.

A tickle ran up his spine. She wasn't responding or indicating that she'd heard or seen him at all. D'Angelo went on the defensive. Either the woman was high, or deeply disturbed. Her right hand came from around her back and rested at her hip. The nails were long and manicured, juxtaposing her ratty wig. He wondered how she did anything with them, especially filed to points like that. Forget using the toilet.

"Alright, let's get moving," he said, trying to hide his frustration. It was times like this that he longed for more female officers on the force. He might have reached out and touched a guy, but he didn't put his hands on women unless he had to. Besides, she smelled atrocious. The sooner he could get her where she needed to go, the better.

The woman could have mental issues or a learning disability. It was best to approach the situation in a calm manner so as not to set her off. "Miss, can you hear me? Do you need help? How about I go to the nurse's station and bring someone here? Would that be okay?" He waited for a sign that she understood.

Her eyes closed for a long beat. He watched her chest rise and fall, slower and deeper each time. An audible sigh escaped her lips. It sounded unnaturally deep. He tapped his bodycam to make sure it was there, although he never put on his uniform without it.

D'Angelo eased around the woman, hoping not to disturb her while he went for help. Besides the rising and falling of her chest, she didn't move. He faced her side, never taking his eyes off her. His pulse pounded in his temples as he slid around her. An immense pressure lifted when he cleared the doorway and entered the freezing hallway.

It appeared darker and greener than it had before. Sweat broke out along his forehead, and he considered that he may have caught a bug from being in the hospital so much lately. He walked the corridor, looking for signs of other officers. Where was everyone?

He switched on his radio, listening for signs of activity, and got an earful of static. The hospital felt cold, as if he were the only soul inhabiting the entire floor. Out of curiosity, he crossed the hall at the nurse's station and went down the corridor parallel to the chief's. There were no officers or nurses in sight.

At least the hall looked clear. He doubled back to the chief's room, finding it the way he'd left it. The chief lay in the bed, unmoved, unbothered. D'Angelo dropped the snacks onto the bed table and emptied the drinks from his pockets. He put on his jacket, glad for the extra layer against the sudden cold. The chief didn't look cold, but he covered him with a thin hospital blanket anyway.

"Be right back, Chief. Gotta check on something. Don't worry, I've got it covered." He patted his boss on the shoulder and left the room.

The man who had been sleeping in the first lounge had left some time ago, and none of the nurses had returned. It seemed strange to not find at least one in any of the rooms along the way, checking charts, temperatures, and such. When he reached the lounge, the woman too was gone. That bothered him, but she hadn't done anything wrong anyway, except not wearing a badge. Something about her bothered him, but he couldn't put his finger on why.

The radio at the nurse's station came on full blast. The thunderous drums of an AC/DC rock classic made him jump out of his skin. "Oh shit," D'Angelo muttered, clutching his chest. No one came to shut it off. He ran behind the station to do it himself, though it felt odd to be on this side of the desk. His fingers fiddled with the sleek silver and blue unit, but he couldn't find the off switch. The music rose to ear-splitting levels, as did his heart rate and blood pressure. He had to stop eating all that damned junk food.

Nothing worked, and it seemed like no one was coming, whether it was to help or complain. He took off his jacket and wrapped it around the box. The volume lessened, but not in any way that was significant. Annoyed, he tossed the whole thing into a file box and shut it. The sound cut down to a mild disturbance. This was ridiculous. He had to find a nurse.

He took off down the hall and the music blasted loud and clear like before. Fucking hell. D'Angelo ran past the second lounge intent on going to the next floor up or down to get someone, and stopped dead in his tracks. The woman in the wig was still there, standing next to the vending machine, a bloodied nurse in her clutches.

D'Angelo drew his piece and pointed it at her. "You sick bitch, let me see your fucking hands!" The woman's eyes were closed, as they had been before. D'Angelo didn't remember her lips or her eyes being criss-crossed in black stitches. "GET YOUR HANDS UP OR I WILL SHOOT YOU."

She let go of the eviscerated nurse and raised her bloodied claws above her head. The nurse plopped to the floor, her heart, drenched in blood blacker than he'd ever seen, sat in the middle of her chest, still beating.

D'Angelo steadied his hands and stepped closer to the woman. "Get on your knees and lock your fingers together behind your head."

The woman did as she was told. Her head tilted as if she could see him through her stitched lids. He bit down on his lip to relieve the itch from the sweat gathered on his upper lip. The woman tilted her head.

"Lay on your stomach," he said. "Now." Unmoved by his insistence the corners of her mouth twitched, tugging at the thick threads until the taut skin stretched. "Don't," he said, more to himself than her.

Were it not for the dead nurse lying at his feet, he would have turned away from the spectacle playing out in front of him. The stitched skin around her mouth ripped free of the threads, separating into loose bits of bloody meat. "God in heaven." D'Angelo dropped his service gun to his side, far too disturbed by her self-mutilation. He didn't know if she needed a bullet or a straitjacket, but he could provide neither.

His body moved backwards until it passed over the threshold and into the hallway. Clouds of condensation escaped his lips, adding to the eerie atmosphere. He backed into the wall and watched the woman's unclasped hands rip open each eyelid. Thick, milky eyes layered in white film peeked at him. Underneath the eggy consistency, red irises sought him out.

D'Angelo slid to the right in the direction of the chief's room. He couldn't stay here looking at that... whatever it was. He refused to believe she was human, looking like something that crawled out of his worst nightmares. And how was she not in pain after what she'd done to herself? No one could withstand such horror, and when had someone done that to her face? He'd left her alone for a mere few minutes and she looked like she'd been the victim of a diabolical botched plastic surgery.

He backed away from the room, making sure she didn't get any ideas to follow him. There needed to be some space between them so that he could find out what the hell had happened to the rest of his officers. When he was certain that she wasn't coming, he did a one-eighty, running right into her. Shocked, he fell flat on the floor. The impact skittered his taser across the smooth surface, into one of the patient's rooms under the bed.

She was on him before his next move materialized in his head. The attack started with her claws slicing through his shirt and undershirt. D'Angelo cried out, terrified and vulnerable. She never made a sound as she made light work of his forearms, his face, his chest.

Blinded by his own blood, he bucked her until he could gain leverage and lift them off the floor. He crashed on top of her, crushing her with his bodyweight. The woman wriggled a hand free and stabbed at the back of his head. D'Angelo reached up and grasped her wrist. Her other hand became free and she backhanded him. He flew farther than he thought possible, slamming into the double doors leading to the floor from the elevators.

Again she pounced, attacking him with her claws. He felt his strength drain from his left arm as she cut into the meat. He kicked at her to avoid her slicing the tendons in his thumb and fingers, which would leave him defenseless without the ability to grasp. She changed tactics and slammed his head into the floor. His body slipped into unconsciousness, but not before he felt the sensation of a heavy weight lifting off of him.

Chapter Fifteen

"Can you tell us what happened again, Sir?" Officer Rosa West, an average-sized, pretty woman of Puerto Rican origin, stood next to Rukhsana with her hands clinging to the bed rails. It was no secret that she had a crush on the detective. Whenever he asked for volunteers, she was first to speak up and take an extra shift, or work a case with him.

Chief Davis liked to tease his daughter, updating her with daily gossip about her competition, Rosa. He had a theory that Detective Wright only liked women whose names started with "R." Rukhsana wished D'Angelo would return Rosa's affections and leave her out of it.

"Yes, Detective, what happened?" Rukhsana asked. She was on the way to her father's room when one of the officers told her about Detective Wright's run-in with a crazed person in the lounge.

"It's like I told you. There was a Black woman, about five foot six, my complexion, with a light brown wig, a blue shirt, and jeans. She didn't say a word to me, Rosa." He winced as a nurse pulled a long thread back and forth through his hand. None of the tendons were severed like he'd imagined, but there was a significant amount of lacerations on his hands, arms, chest, the back of his head, and face. She cut the thread after one final pass, and bandaged his hand. He wasn't pretty right now, but the nurse promised he would be when the stitches healed. "Thank you, nurse."

"You're welcome." The nurse put away her scissors, bandages, and gauze. "I'll send someone over with some more pain medication for you. You can shower if you feel like it in a couple of days."

"A couple of days?" D'Angelo winced. "I won't have many visitors if I wait that long."

"Your real friends will," Officer West said, smiling.

Rukhsana closed her eyes to keep from rolling them. She felt like she was about to become Officer West's third wheel as the nurse left.

"You said she wasn't wearing a visitor's badge?" Rosa asked.

"No, she wasn't. I thought she might be lost or special needs, or God knows what, so I went down the hall to get some help. None of the nurses were on the floor, and neither were our officers."

"Hmm," Rosa said, peering at the detective.

"What's on your mind, Rosa?"

Officer West glanced at Rukhsana, then at the detective.

"It's okay. Rukhsana is family," Detective Wright said.

"Chief Davis is family," Rosa said, cutting her eyes at Rukhsana.

Detective Wright sighed. "Either way, she's here, and I want her to brought up to speed. She's acting as a consultant, since this might be related to the incident she and the chief had."

"On whose authority?" Rosa asked, crossing her arms.

"Mine," Detective Wright said.

That was news to Rukhsana. She hadn't spoken to the detective since she went home yesterday afternoon, and now she was consulting on the hospital case? Whatever had happened, she was going to need a thorough explanation.

Officer West sighed. "Well, there are surveillance cameras set up all along the floor. If we can get those tapes, we can see who the woman is then find her. Also, with your delicate condition, you're gonna need someone to run the station."

"No, I'm don't. There are protocols in place while I'm away from the station, but I'm getting out of here tonight."

"But you need to rest," Officer West protested.

"I agree with her, Detective. You've been through some type of ordeal. Let the others handle the station for a while. Lord knows you're always stepping up for my dad."

"What do you know about the Lord?"

Rukhsana's head snapped in Rosa's direction. "Excuse me?" she asked, shivering. The temperature had plummeted.

"That was rude, Rosa," Detective Wright said, wrinkling his nose. Rukhsana smelled it too. Sulfur.

"Do you think this bitch has God on her side?" The voices came out distorted. She's too arrogant, too dependent on her toys and tricks to stop us," Officer West said.

"Rosa?" Detective Wright sat up. "What's going on?"

Blood poured from the officer's nose. She backed away from the bed and stuck out her tongue, lapping up the flow. "You're gonna burn in hell very soon like your mother," Rosa said, facing Rukhsana. "The best is yet to come, Rukhsana. We're gonna destroy you, and everyone else that loves you."

Rukhsana took a step backwards and reached into her sweater pocket for the small vial of Zamzam water she had brought with her. She popped the top and shook it at Officer West. "Bismillahir Rahmanir Raheem." The multiple voices screeched. Officer West clawed at her face. Rukhsana flung more water at her until the woman doubled over and vomited on the floor.

"Oh my God," Detective Wright said, watching in disbelief from the bed as the vomit crawled across the floor towards Rukhsana. The vial emptied, she stood her ground, continuing her recitation. "Bismillah." Rukhsana spat three times on the congealed mass until it caught alight. They watched it burn until it turned to ash. "Alhamdulillah, it's destroyed," Rukhsana said.

"Santo Dios, that was inside me?" Officer West said, crossing herself. "I need to see a priest. I think I'm gonna throw up again." She hunched over the sink and retched.

Rukhsana turned on the tap and directed her to wash her face. Officer West gave her a grateful look, then bent over the sink.

"We're gonna need those security tapes," Detective Wright said.

"No need." They all turned to the officer standing in the doorway. "Sorry to bother you, Detective. I think we found the woman you were talking about."

"Good work, Michaels. Where is she?"

Officer Michaels hesitated. "You really need to come and see for yourself, Sir."

"HOW IN THE hell is this possible?" Detective Wright said, gathering his IV drip stand and moving closer. "She was wearing street clothes and standing in the family lounge." He leaned over the woman and studied the scars on her face. "She killed a nurse."

"Detective, she's been in a medically induced coma for weeks," Doctor Coleman said. "Poor thing had just come from the clinic downstairs—domestic dispute with her boyfriend when she got hit by a bus.

"Does she have a twin?" Officer West asked.

"Not likely," the doctor said.

"Maybe something or someone was impersonating her," Detective Wright said. "The way she killed that nurse—we need to find out which nurse is missing, by the way."

"Let's not jump to conclusions," the doctor said. "All my nurses are accounted for. Besides, we should wait for the tapes, but I don't have to tell you guys that, you're the cops." He forced a laugh. "How about we let the patient rest and figure this out somewhere else."

A throng of footsteps pounded the hallway and stopped outside the patient's room. It was Officer Michaels and two other deputies. "What's going on?" Detective Wright asked.

"Chief Davis is not in his bed," one of the deputies said.

"What do you mean, the chief is missing?" Detective Wright asked.

"My father's not in his hospital bed, D'Angelo. You promised to watch over him, and now he's gone missing. I thought that I could count on you." Rukhsana wrung her hands together to keep from placing them around the detective's neck. She hated to kick a man when he was down, and he certainly was looking more dead than alive if she were honest, but the whole operation had turned into a shit show. "Where is he?"

Rukhsana tore through the deputies, not waiting for an answer. She entered the stairway at the end of the hall and climbed to the ICU floor as fast as her body would take her. Her heart pounded as she halted outside her father's hospital room. There were several nurses crowded around his empty bed. "Where is he? Where's my dad?" The elevator doors opened and Detective Wright stepped out with Officers West and Michaels behind him.

"We're gonna need you to calm down, Rukhsana, this is the ICU," one of the nurses said.

"How could you lose a man in a coma? Was it too much trouble to watch him? Is he not worth your time?" She threw her hands up, frustrated and likely on the verge of getting kicked out, but she didn't care what they thought of her, she wanted her dad.

"Please calm down, we will find him," another nurse said, approaching her.

"I want this place searched top to bottom or you'll have a hell of a lawsuit on your hands," she said.

"I need everyone to stay calm," Detective Wright said, entering the room. His jacket, retrieved from the file cabinet earlier, sat loosely over his hospital gown. "I need men on every floor searching every room, lounge, and bathroom. West, take the top floor, Michaels, go to the morgue, the rest of you hit all the floors in between. Let's move."

"You're in no condition to search," Officer West said to the detective.

"I'm well enough to walk. It's you who should take a breather if you need one," he said.

"I'm good, Detective. Chief Davis is family, remember?" Officer West jutted out her chin, determined to remain close.

"I'm coming with you," Rukhsana said.

"You should stay here in case he comes back. We don't know if he walked out on his own," Officer West said.

"How could he do that if he's in a coma?"

"What's going on?" Doctor Ahmed broke through the pack of

police officers and entered the room. "Where's your dad? Did some-thing happen to him?"

"Naureen, he's missing. I don't know if someone has taken him or if he's hurt somewhere. I can't take much more of this," Rukhsana said, not fighting her tears. Her friend's presence made her feel safe enough to drop her tough facade.

"Hey, it's alright, Roxie. We'll find him." Naureen took her in a comforting embrace. Rukhsana winced from her injuries which had started down the slow road to healing.

"We're heading upstairs," Detective Wright said. "I'll call you if we find him."

Rukhsana broke from her friend's embrace. "Naureen, can you stay here? I want to go to the chapel."

"Someone is checking the main floor," Officer West said.

"I know. But there's another one upstairs that the hospital doesn't use anymore. Dad used to sneak in there when my mother got hurt." She squeezed Naureen's hand and left the room.

"I can send someone," Detective Wright said, stepping into the hall after her. "He might need assistance."

"I'm a nurse, D'Angelo. If he's there, I'll call you. You go on and search with Officer West. I'll be fine."

"Alright. Call me if you see anything."

"I will."

$\sim$

THE HOSPITAL'S top floor had served as the administration floor, hosting the gift shop and chapel while the main floor underwent reno-vations over the past two years. Now the floor served as overflow for paper medical records awaiting a scan into the hospital network data-base. A handful of admin worked the floor, mostly manning phones and digging through the records.

Two individuals were stationed at the reception desk as Rukhsana made her way down the corridor towards the chapel. She disliked visiting this place as it brought back painful memories of the days and nights she had spent with her father, watching her mother's slow decline. The stained glass windows portraying picturesque landscapes with rolling hills and rivers cast colorful jewel-toned patterns onto the entrance floor. Strangely, it sent shivers down her spine.

The trees atop the undulating hills appeared to project shadows when viewed from a precise angle. Try as she might, she could never persuade anyone else to notice or acknowledge this phenomenon, which left her wondering if it were all in her head. To her, it appeared that unsavory entities lurked behind those shadows and were looking for ways to break into the material world. She could only imagine what Naureen might say if she heard that.

She pushed open the chapel door while deliberately avoided looking at the stained glass. As she entered the chapel, she found it engulfed in darkness, a stark contrast to its usual well-lit ambiance with light streaming onto the podium on the small stage and above the rows of pews. Alongside the single-row pews, a spacious carpet, accompanied by a stand that held prayer rugs, pointed towards Makkah. In the dimly lit room, a blanketed figure faced her.

"Abi? Is that you?" She reached out to find the light switch, but something obstructed her way. Suspended from various points on the ceiling, several objects hung. In the darkness, she couldn't discern their shapes, but she assumed they were streamers, possibly remnants from previous staff parties held in the mostly unused chapel.

"We've been looking for you. Why didn't you ask for help instead of wandering around when you woke up?" The figure moved in odd intervals until she was no longer convinced that she was looking at her father. She peered at it, scrutinizing it until it stopped moving altogether. The air grew tense as she tried making sense of it. "Abi?"

The figure stood stock-still, not acknowledging her. Were her eyes playing tricks on her? When the hospital was purchased from the Catholic church many years ago by the state, the statues had been hidden away in the storage room. She was going to feel foolish if she'd mistaken her father for a statue.

Again, she reached for the light switch, this time tangling her fingers in between the strange rope-like apparatus and extending as far as she could. "Gotcha," she said, flicking the switch. The lights came up and her hands flew to her mouth. What the naked eye hadn't seen in the dark now became clear.

The doors shut behind her with a soft thud, followed by the click of the latch. In front of her, there was no statue. The figure was a black, misshapen blob. It grew and morphed into something resembling a human, arms and legs protruding from a tar-like substance. The thing grew skin, hair, facial features. Clothing. *A red dress.* She'd never seen a demon do this before.

Rukhsana delved into her pocket, but the entity before her let out a piercing scream, driving her to clamp her hands over her ears as the cries shut down her senses. She tumbled to the floor, unable to bear the noise. Her vision turned white, and she began slipping out of consciousness. Amidst the turmoil, a thudding noise echoed in the background. The banging increased, layering itself underneath the devilish wails.

"Break the glass, break it!" Shattered glass fell around Rukhsana. The demon screeched and went up in a ball of smokeless flames, then disappeared. "Holy God." Officer West peeked in at Rukhsana. "What the hell was that?" She reached through the broken glass and opened the doors from the inside.

Rukhsana gathered her abaya so as not to trip over it when she stood. "My head is killing me," she said.

Officer West helped her to her feet. "What the hell happened here? Who did all this?" The women took in the diabolical embellishments strewn throughout the chapel. Black candles and cloth lay on the small tabernacle and a miniature inverted cross.

"Black mass?" Rukhsana asked, looking over the table's contents.

"They tried," Officer West said. "Whoever did this is an amateur. The upside-down cross is actually a symbol of St. Peter. Real Satanists use other symbols. I don't know what these are though," she said, pointing at the knotted ropes hanging from the ceiling.

"It's called 'uqdah.' Knots that are tied with a spell bound in each one. In English, it's called a witch's ladder. All kinds of spells are used in them. These look pretty sinister to me. Don't touch it. They will need to be removed with gloves and thrown into the incinerator."

"That thing... was it a different demon than the one that got inside me?" Officer West asked. She held her stomach and appeared ill.

"Yes. I've never encountered one like it before."

"What does it want?"

"To destroy us all. Why did you come to the chapel anyway?"

"We found your dad."

Cautious relief washed over her. "Is he alright?"

Officer West shrugged. "He's still in a coma."

"Where'd you find him?"

"In his hospital bed."

"Huh?"

CHAPTER SIXTEEN

"I DON'T GET IT. How could dad disappear from his bed, go missing, then reappear in his bed without anyone noticing?"

"I haven't the faintest idea," Naureen said. She rode home with Rukhsana after they were certain the chief was well-guarded and stabilized in his hospital bed. Detective Wright refused to leave his room, and Officer West promised to come back after she visited a priest on the main floor.

The upstairs chapel was off limits to everyone now that it was a crime scene. It would be some time before anyone worked up enough nerve to enter the space, anyway. The forensics team had gone in and taken out all of the offensive artifacts. A small spectacle had transpired between the team and a zealous admin who argued that the Church of Satan had a right to hang religious regalia in the interfaith chapel like anyone else. It got heated to the point that the admin was taken to the station for questioning.

"Dad couldn't have gotten out of his bed and back in his condition. Some___ 's playing around and I intend to find out who it is."

___ou ever consider that your dad might not be in a coma?"

___na gripped the steering wheel and peered at her friend. As

___as careful and didn't take heavy drugs, driving wasn't out of the question, but all of the tension made her regret getting behind the wheel. "What are you talking about, Naureen? You think he's faking it?"

"It's a possibility. He's gone through severe trauma. Perhaps he's acting out."

"Acting out?" Rukhsana clenched her jaw. While she cherished her bond with Naureen, she couldn't help but resent her scientific viewpoints. They consistently contradicted Rukhsana's own, making it seem as though her friend had adopted science as a means to bolster her arguments and render them unquestionable.

Naureen shrugged. "Yeah. It could be a cry for help."

"Did you forget that I'm a nurse?" Rukhsana asked, turning into their neighborhood.

"Your point?"

"My point, Doctor Naureen, Ph.D, is I watched the nurses perform a series of tests to confirm his coma, and yes, it was confirmed. Didn't you see how his arms fell when they lifted them above his head and let go? He hit himself in the face. No person faking it would do that. Their arms would fall to the side. It's a classic test."

Naureen fell silent as they pulled into her driveway. The passenger door flung open before the car came to a full stop.

Rukhsana's shoulders dropped. "Oh, Lord. Don't tell me that you're mad at me again."

"Why wouldn't I be? You're such an asshole lately, I can't stand it. Don't bother getting out. I'm not inviting you inside my home." Naureen gathered her things and slammed the door. Rukhsana, caught between anger and sadness, sighed and waited until her friend opened the door and turned on the light. Instead, Naureen gave her the finger, entered the dark house, and slammed the door. She never bothered turning on the lights. Rukhsana shook her head and went home.

WHEN SHE WALKED through the door, she paused, assessing the atmosphere. Relieved that nothing seemed out of place, and that her home wasn't under siege, she closed the door and hung up her sweater. She turned on the lights as she went, electric bill be damned.

It wasn't right to live alone. There should be some signs of life in the home besides one's own. What would Abi say when he came home and perhaps found a couple of kittens pawing at the furniture, or some budgies singing love songs in a cage?

A part of her questioned whether he *would* return home, or if he had rested on his pillow for the final time a few days ago. That part of her felt weary. The struggle to meet the ever-growing spiritual demands had been challenging, and now that the otherworldly had materialized in the physical realm, she found herself overwhelmed and struggled to maintain a positive outlook. She longed for someone to talk to.

There was nothing she desired more than to find solace in someone's comforting presence when the weight of her burdens became too much. However, she couldn't help but consider it selfish. Sharing her experiences of spiritual intrusion with a partner could potentially put that person in harm's way.

Then there was her absence of sexual longing. That would be a deal-breaker for any partner. Naureen assured her that it was rooted in her fears, and that if she abandoned exorcisms, her innate desires would reawaken. What Naureen couldn't grasp was that she had never possessed desires to begin with.

She sat on the edge of her bed and hugged herself. There was always Victor for conversation. Her poor cousin. He had tried reaching out to her, but she had brushed him off. She owed him the biggest apology the next time they spoke.

A moment of inspiration sparked the perfect apology. Flowers. Victor would appreciate the gesture, with his love of floriography, and all things cryptic.

After a quick web search for the most appropriate flowers to send a man for an apology, she scrolled through pages of flowers for sale on a local Rosewood Hollow florist's website and bought him a big bouquet of white roses, with an apology note attached. In the morning, she'd give him a call.

He deserved more, considering how upset he had sounded. And what had he been trying to tell her? Something about how the family was under duress, and that someone was coming after them. If he only knew half of it. For every human enemy, there were hundreds of supernatural ones. The battle of the soul only ends with death.

Her cellphone rang. She checked the caller and sucked in a breath. "Hello, Detective. Is my dad okay?"

"Don't worry, Rukhsana, he's sleeping soundly. I'm sorry to bother you, I know you just got home."

"About five minutes ago," she said, massaging her neck.

"Yeah, I figured. Listen, I'm calling because I'm concerned for you. Rosa told me what she saw in the chapel."

"Oh, that. Listen, I'm okay, I've seen worse."

"That's just it, Rukhsana. I've never seen anything like what we've experienced today, and it is freaking me the hell out. I don't understand how you can be taking it so calmly. This is some devilish shit that I'm not prepared for."

"D'Angelo, listen. My father and I are used to seeing things like this. We perform exorcisms for parishioners all the time. Well, we used to before my mother died."

"See, I know all that because your mother told me. She also said that —" he fell silent.

"Said what?"

"Nothing. I'm concerned."

"I appreciate that. There's nothing you can do but pray for me and my father, and that is plenty." She listened to him breathe on the other end and waited. He seemed on the verge of telling her something and she didn't want to rush it.

"I wish you had someone to confide in."

"I have Naureen."

"Besides her," he said, not hiding his irritation.

"Why do you say that? She's like a sister to me."

"Do you feel obligated to put up with her bullshit because your family took her in?"

"Excuse me?"

"I don't mean to speak ill of her, but I've seen you two argue, and I wonder if you invest too much of yourself in making sure she's living a normal life?"

"I care for Naureen. We're all she's got. Her entire family live across the country and act like she never existed."

"I know, the chief told me. But ask yourself, when do you start living for yourself? You can't be everything for someone else, Rukhsana."

"You make it sound like I don't have a life of my own."

"Do you? Aren't you wondering what lies ahead?"

"None of us can tell the future, D'Angelo."

"No, but we all worry about our careers and personal lives. I mean, speaking for myself, I feel like I'm at an age where I want to find someone special to share my life with. Don't you want that too? Your mother told me how hard it was for her and your father when they found out—"

She perked up. "When they found out what?"

"Sorry, my other phone is ringing. I have to take the call, it's for a case. I'll call you tomorrow." The phone went dead, and Rukhsana sat there wondering what he was talking about, and why her mother had confided in him so much in her last days. She called Naureen to discuss it, but the phone went straight to voicemail. She found another local florist and ordered a bouquet of buttery-yellow tulips for Naureen. The card read, 'Sorry for being an asshole.'

Chapter Seventeen

Officer West kept glancing over her shoulder as she waited for the basement elevator to take her up to the ICU floor. The unsettling security guard had rattled her nerves, but the whole floor gave her the creeps. Any peace her visit with the priest had brought evaporated the moment she stepped down there. Why had she volunteered to fetch this damn tape after already heading home for the night? Because D'Angelo needed it—and deep down, she wanted him to need her too. She just hoped the tight jeans she'd squeezed into weren't wasted on the security guard.

Every little favor, every task she volunteered for kept her in the forefront of his mind. At least, it would have if the chief's daughter would stay out of the way. She harbored a strong dislike for Rukhsana, and suspected that there was more to the story than what she had told D'Angelo in his report.

The girl was bad news. She'd been the one to report her mother missing the night they found her buried under all that rubble, and now her father had been seriously injured, and two good cops were dead. If she had her way, she'd be investigating her.

When the elevator finally arrived, she jumped inside and pressed the button for the fourth floor repeatedly until the doors closed. She breathed a sigh of relief when the car started moving. As much as she wanted to be at D'Angelo's side, she couldn't deny that some time away from work was in order.

She wasn't a stranger to the supernatural, although it had been quite some time since she had last encountered it. Whatever was unfolding within this hospital wouldn't resolve itself; a spiritual intervention was necessary. Her family would have the knowledge to guide her if she reached out. Some of them shared her Catholic faith, but the majority were practitioners of brujeria.

Her mother had vehemently opposed her becoming a witch, which had led them to move away from their extended family in New York. When she found a promising job in Virginia, she relocated them once more, leaving behind any ties to Puerto Rico, and assimilating into the predominantly white Catholic community in Salem, Virginia. Unbeknownst to her mother, Virginia had its own rich history of witchcraft, which Rosa occasionally delved into out of curiosity.

What had started as a mere curiosity had evolved into an almost obsessive interest, much like her feelings for D'Angelo. Her mother wouldn't approve of either; no black magic, and no Black men. She wondered if her past explorations had made her a potential target for spiritual entities.

She trembled, recalling the evil spirit taking on a physical form as she expelled it from her body. The vivid and unsettling images had haunted her throughout the night, making sleep elusive. Drained and irritated by her restless evening, she got dressed and informed D'Angelo that she was willing to head down to the basement security hub to retrieve the surveillance tapes.

The guard had leered at her while he copied the video onto an external hard drive she'd given him. She was used to it; men were often taken with her beauty. Maybe that's why she wanted D'Angelo so badly; he didn't seem to notice her at all. The elevator doors dinged. She told herself that all it would take was a little more time before he'd be chasing her harder than any man ever had.

"Good morning, Detective. I thought you'd be in the chief's room," Rosa said, entering Detective Wright's hospital room. "Sneaked you some junk food."

"Rosa? Why aren't you sleeping? It's three in the morning." The detective smiled. He was sitting on the bed, cross-legged, clicking through case files in the department's online database. "Thank you," he said, accepting the bag of doughnuts. "I tried signing myself out, and the damned nurses bullied me into staying. I'm getting out of here at about ten, thank God."

"No, you should stay as long as you can. Nobody wants you relapsing when the chief is incapacitated. What would we do without you both?"

"That's sweet of you to say, but I'm sure you'd survive. You're a good cop."

"I'm a good friend, too, D'Angelo." She pulled up a chair. "The feed starts with the last hour and works its way backwards on the security footage. The guards in this place are real creeps. I almost had to promise the guy a date to get it," she said, holding up a flash drive.

"Seriously? You'd think the scumbag could respect the situation we're in and not hit on you."

"I know. It's alright. I did what I had to do for you. I want you to know that," she said, looking deeply into his eyes.

"Rosa," he said, shifting on the bed.

"Yes?" She loved it when he said her name. Dropping the formalities between them made her feel more connected. *Seen.*

"I appreciate how you've gone above and beyond the call of duty for the chief—"

"I did it for you. So that you wouldn't have to worry about anything while you're healing."

"I don't know how to thank you," he said, inserting the flash drive into the computer.

"You could take me out to dinner." She sat still, allowing her words to linger in the silence.

"Like I said, I appreciate you, Rosa, but I'm interested in Rukhsana."

His words punched her in the gut. She knew how he felt, but to hear him say it aloud grated on her. "What's so special about her? Are you chasing after her because she's the chief's daughter? Everybody knows she's weird. She hangs out with that shrink doctor who's just as strange. It wouldn't surprise me if those two had some kind of twisted thing going on."

Detective Wright snapped to attention. "Watch your mouth. That's the chief's daughter, and she's a respectable woman."

Rosa folded her arms. "Wake up, Detective, or you're gonna die alone."

"If I do, it's my decision." He stared at the computer screen in disbelief and drew in a sharp breath.

Rosa dropped her arms. "What is it? Detective?" She moved closer, studying the screen. "Oh my God, is that the chief?"

"What is he doing?" the detective asked. "What's he spitting into her mouth?"

"Oh God. D'Angelo, he's killing her."

Detective Wright jumped off the bed, slipped into his jacket, and grabbed his service weapon. Officer West followed.

CHAPTER EIGHTEEN

RUKHSANA AWOKE to a dark bedroom lit by a lone streetlamp. The power had failed. She leaned over and picked up her cellphone. It hadn't been charged. The analog alarm clock she kept ticked faithfully in the dark. She didn't need visual confirmation to know what time it was. When she finally looked, she was right. Three A.M.

She sat up and rubbed the sleep from her eyes. A simmering undercurrent of anger threatened to surface, though she recognized it as fatigue. A childhood lesson from her mother resurfaced in her thoughts: *There are no breaks for the strong.* Despite her weariness, she understood she hadn't yet reached her limits. As a devoted servant of God, she believed that her trials were tailored to her strength.

If that's true, why did Ummi die? The intrusive thought left her feeling dirty. She murmured a prayer and spat lightly over her shoulder three times, more of a tongue-flick than a liquid expiation, to chase off lesser malevolent spirits who whispered negative thoughts into her psyche.

When the fog lifted, she got off the bed and went to the window. It was late, but there was always someone awake. Down the street, she saw lights burning in windows and sighed. The power failure was only at her house. *Typical.*

A strange scent drifted upstairs, as if someone were trying to cook food that had just crossed the line into spoiled territory. She donned a hijab and grabbed her Qur'an and a vial of Zamzam. Then she went to her closet and unlocked her gun box. Holy water was one thing, but it was best to take every precaution with a murderer on the loose.

HER FEET MOVED DOWN the carpeted staircase, careful of the creaky spots. Breathing came with great difficulty as the kitchen came into view. Fear gripped her ribcage, halting each breath in her chest. *But the smell.* The putrid odor made her not want to breathe at all.

Whoever was in there was at the far end where she couldn't see them. The distinct sound of chopping put her on edge. She wiped her sweaty palms and readjusted the grip on her handgun, hoping she wouldn't have to use it.

It had been some time since she'd been to the shooting range. In all honesty, she didn't know if she had it in her to put a bullet into a person. Her job was to draw out evil, not incapacitate people, or kill them.

As her foot landed on the hard floor in the hall before the kitchen, she moved to the side of the doorway and peered inside. The entire room had been upturned. There were mixing bowls filled with bloody contents she couldn't identify, and something sizzled on a pan. A large stock pot overflowed on the left back burner. She could see the outline of its contents bobbing up and down in the pot. A head of some sort.

"They say if you boil a pig's head, the meat and fat cook down nicely for soups and meat jelly. I've never done it before, but I owed you a meal and thought I'd experiment, you know?"

A portion of Rukhsana's vitality appeared to ebb away, leaving her frail within the vessel that contained her soul. Her hands lowered, and she closed her eyes. *It's not more than you can handle. It's not more than you can handle.*

Despite her inner monologue's reassurances, her eyes welled with tears. She mentally rewound the years, finding herself sixteen years in the past, feeling twenty all over again. She was on winter break from college, visiting Naureen at Dominion Springs, a mental institution in Rosewood Hollow.

In their final session of ruqya, Rukhsana had watched Naureen recite Qur'an from memory with no adverse reactions. She had exhibited no difficulty performing her prayers throughout the day, and her doctors had complimented her consistently uplifted mood. It had been a perfect exorcism—perhaps too perfect.

Rukhsana had misgivings, but her parents seemed to think their daughter's gift had brought about a miraculous transformation in the young woman. They refused to let her doubt her divine abilities and insisted on serving as mentors to Naureen as she approached her eighteenth birthday and her release from the institution.

Upon release, they found her a job, cosigned her apartment, and lauded her entry to school on a full scholarship. Thanks to a rigorous correspondence program, she transferred into Rosewood Hollow University with two years under her belt.

"I know what you're thinking," Naureen said, cutting away in the kitchen. "You're thinking about how your parents hyped you up all those years ago. That all those years of forced Qur'an lessons, constant revisions of your memorization, and mock exorcisms hadn't come to fruition the way they said it would. You're feeling like the biggest fraud on the planet right now, am I right?"

Rukhsana kept the gun in her left hand and reached into her right pocket and rubbed the cover until it squeaked.

"Don't tell me you still carry that little book? I think we can both agree that it hasn't done its job," Naureen said, setting the knife on the counter.

"Naureen, what are you doing?"

Naureen clapped her hands together. Rukhsana jumped. "Cooking for you, silly. I told you that I'd make you a meal when you felt better."

She turned around and Rukhsana saw black pits in the place where Naureen's eyes used to be. Naureen picked up the cutting board and presented it.

Rukhsana dropped to her knees. Her fingers loosened and the firearm slipped free. "Audhubillah, Naureen, what did you do to your eyes?"

"Deviled them. I added some chopped red onion and paprika the way you like. There's dill, too."

Now was not the time to get light-headed or fade to black. Instead, Rukhsana clutched her stomach and settled for a good old-fashioned puke.

Chapter Nineteen

"Dammit, he's gone again. Michaels, get everyone and search every room on this floor."

"Come on, Wright," Michaels complained. "We can't keep doing this. He's one guy."

"Excuse me, officers, what's going on?" A nurse from the ward asked.

"We've got a situation," Detective Wright said. "Tell your nurses who are at the station to remain there. The others who are working with patients are to remain in the rooms until we've cleared this floor."

"Wright, it's three in the morning. I haven't heard shit from any of the rooms all night," Michaels said. He'd been taking on double shifts, figuring there'd be plenty of money rolling in for minimal effort, but the extended hours were taking a toll. "He'll come back on his own. It's obvious the nurses are the ones losing him."

Officer West holstered her weapon and pushed her finger into the complaining deputy's chest. "Move your ass, Michaels, and don't give me any shit. The chief's in one of these rooms doing God knows what. We need to find him right away, now move!"

Michaels turned beet red, grumbled something under his breath, and led two deputies on a hunt from room to room down the corridor.

"Thanks, Rosa."

"Let's check the other side, Detective," Officer West said. "Try not to let your love for the chief and his daughter cloud your judgment. Whole family's fucked up," she said, turning the corner.

"Check down that way, and I'll go down here," he said, ignoring her. He couldn't believe she'd turn on the chief because D'Angelo had feelings for his daughter. None of that mattered now. They had to find him. And then what? He hoped to God that he'd been mistaken about what he'd witnessed on the security feed. There had to be a logical explanation, though he couldn't begin to fathom what it might be.

The current circumstances were beyond both his professional training and his grasp of the real world. D'Angelo had heard about Rukhsana's involvement in spiritual matters at her family's mosque, but he had assumed it was merely counseling for congregants in need.

Raised in the Catholic school system by atheist parents who had primarily chosen it for the education and free meals provided by the nuns, faith had never been a part of his life. He had always thought he could address his lack of spiritual practice when the time came to propose to Rukhsana. However, he now understood the depth of his misconception and felt completely lost, unsure of how to move forward.

What the hell was he supposed to do with the chief? The man had been the father figure he'd needed all his life, and now he was mauling patients like a rabid dog? He didn't know if he'd hesitate when the time came to confront his mentor, or shoot him dead on the spot. D'Angelo hoped to the chief's God that he wouldn't have to deliver more than a flesh wound. That way, Rukhsana could work her spiritual healing and rid her dad of the evil wreaking havoc on him and spare the rest of the patients.

He moved from room to room, finding nurses in some, quietly changing linens, giving sponge baths, and administering medications. As he approached the final room, he secretly hoped the chief wouldn't be found at all—that the sight of his hero attacking a patient had been nothing more than a disturbing hallucination. In the last room, Dr. Coleman was comforting a grieving family gathered around their recently deceased loved one. D'Angelo sighed with relief.

"Detective, he's here," Officer West called.

"I'm coming, Rosa." D'Angelo darted into the hall. Officer West stood outside a room with her weapon at the ready.

"Chief, get your hands up where I can see them," she said, charging into the room before he could stop her.

"Rosa, wait. Rosa, dammit, don't shoot him!" Detective Wright sprinted down the hall, scrambling to prevent Officer West from committing a regrettable act. He slid into the doorway, relieved that she hadn't emptied her weapon into the man. D'Angelo saw why. The chief had his back turned to her.

"Chief, it's me, D'Angelo. Turn around and put your hands up." He winced at the gnashing and growling sounds coming from the chief. His large frame hid most of the carnage, but the red-splattered walls and soaking sheets that dripped onto the floor filled in the blanks. The room smelled of rotten eggs and blood.

"Santo Dios, Holy Mary... Chief?" Officer West approached Chief Davis from the bedside near the door while D'Angelo took up a position on the opposite side. D'Angelo gestured for her to stay back, reluctant to disrupt the chief from his apparent trance.

Seeing the horror for himself, D'Angelo gagged, stepped back, and gagged again. The patient, what was left of them, lay open from the chest down, skin and organs nowhere insight. There was nothing inside the corpse's cavity as far as he could tell, and he for sure didn't want to know where the missing parts were. The ribs reminded him of a prepared rack of lamb.

"Chief," D'Angelo said, his voice shaking. "Goddamn it, look at me." He got his wish. The agonizingly slow way that Chief Davis turned towards him sent a chill down his spine and nausea swirled in his gut. Pointed teeth and ashen skin rendered the man unrecognizable. He didn't seem human in this demonic state.

He regretted his initial decision to handle the chief without using weapons. After his incident with the woman in the lounge, D'Angelo considered whether he'd be able to draw his gun from its holster before Chief Davis attacked. He didn't think so.

"Chief, something bad has happened to you. I don't know what it is, or how to explain it, but you've gotta trust me. I'm not going to hurt you. Climb down from there and let me help you." The chief's body twitched. His head began oscillating like a serpent's, undulating and tracking him. The whites of his eyes had turned a deep crimson, as if filled with blood, while his piercing electric blue pupils seemed to burn holes into the detective.

"He's not listening, Detective. I think we need to subdue him," Officer West said.

"Stay back, Rosa. Let me try to handle this without violence."

"Are you insane? Detective, he's ripped this guy to shreds with his bare hands. Hell, I can't even say for sure that it is a guy. I say we shoot him before he—" Rosa cried out. The chief had moved faster than D'Angelo's eyes could register. D'Angelo winced at the sounds of crunching bones and popping ligaments. The chief turned Officer West's head until D'Angelo could see her chin sitting flush between her shoulder blades in the sink mirror behind them.

"Rosa, oh no, no." D'Angelo removed his weapon from the holster and aimed.

"No, don't you do it, don't you—" Doctor Coleman stood in the doorway. The chief flew across the room, landing on the doctor. D'Angelo stared in horror as did the doctor. "...shoooot in heeere," the freed vocal cords vibrated in the chief's bloody fist.

The definitive sound of bullets emptying from D'Angelo's weapon filled the room. Black blood splattered the white walls and bedding as the chief crumpled to the floor. D'Angelo squeezed the trigger long after he emptied his revolver.

From the corner of his eye, he saw Officer West's body, head still twisted, rise from the floor.

"Rosa?" She turned around until her back faced him. Her eyes opened. A sinister smile flashed across her face before she took off running towards the stairs. Stunned for a moment, D'Angelo hesitated before chasing after her, this time with his weapon drawn. Nurses screamed in the corridor behind him. Deputies shouted for them to clear a path and let them through.

"Go on without us, Wright. We'll catch up," Michaels yelled through the chaos. The nurses and visitors continued filling the hall, blocking the police. D'Angelo continued on without backup.

CHAPTER TWENTY

"AUDHUBILLAHI MIN ASH shaytan ir rajeem. Bismillah ar-Rahman ar-Raheem. In the name of Allah, Most Gracious, Most Merciful."

Rukhsana and Naureen circled the kitchen island, both keeping a steady pace, avoiding getting within each other's reach. Rukhsana grabbed the buffalo-checked kitchen towel hanging from the oven door then used it to swipe everything within reach from the countertop. She kicked the butchered swine parts that littered the floor out of the way with her slippers. She didn't want anything in her way. This was going to end today.

"Why are you doing that? That's good meat," Naureen said in a voice that was not her own. Rukhsana instantly recognized it. Once again, she was given a chilling reminder of the hellish days she spent fervently extracting demons from her best friend. Here they were, full circle; the same two girls against the same demon. A sense of sorrow washed over Rukhsana as she moved around the counter, sprinkling Zamzam water in her path. Naureen's soles sizzled, leaving a gruesome bloody trail on the floor as she kept pace. Before long, it became difficult to tell who was chasing whom.

t was too soon for a crisis of confidence, but she couldn't shake the questions of why and how the demon had managed to survive. There was no doubt they had defeated it, yet here it was, inside her friend. With a swift movement, Rukhsana pulled open a drawer on the kitchen island, retrieving a tightly bundled rope and a larger bottle of water.

"Come here, bitch," Naureen snarled. She swiftly appeared around the corner, prompting Rukhsana to quicken her pace, leaving the drawer ajar to block her pursuit.

The drawer slammed shut, propelled by an unseen force. Rukhsana looped the rope over her arm and unscrewed the cap on the Zamzam bottle. She then scattered it across the counter, bleaching the pig's blood on the towel stark white as she feverishly wiped the grimy surface.

"Naureen, I know you're in there," Rukhsana said as she began unwrapping the rope, "we're gonna get you back, once and for all."

Her friend's hijacked body switched up and changed direction, surprising Rukhsana. She flung some of the water at Naureen, driving her away, once again forcing her to circumambulate counterclockwise at a slow and steady pace, like a wicked mockery of a pilgrim's trek around the Ka'bah.

This was a technique her mother had imparted when she was a little girl, just beginning her training. The direction left weaker demons disoriented and ineffective. More formidable shayateen, such as the one inhabiting Naureen, might become unsettled, giving Rukhsana time to gather her composure.

Rukhsana kept up the pace a little longer, unraveled more of the rope, tying it into a lasso, then slowed her pace. Naureen closed the distance between them. Rukhsana spun on her heels, flinging the rope over her friend. Naureen fought against the ties; the more she struggled, the tighter it became. "Bismillah, in the name of the Lord of All the Worlds, I command you to leave this body," Rukhsana began.

"Don't worry, the way this whore is built, there won't be much body left when I'm done with her," the demon gloated.

"She's tougher than you are or she wouldn't have survived all your attempts to break her," Rukhsana said. The demon's gaze penetrated her heart through Naureen's empty eye sockets. Rukhsana shuddered but quickly regained her composure, more resolved than ever to exorcise the monster.

That malicious expression had appeared on her friend's face many times during their youth. She was frightened, but not because of that. Her friend, once so strong over the years, had somehow had her defenses stripped away completely by a jinni that was powerful, yet not so strong that Rukhsana doubted she hadn't defeated it all those years ago.

"I don't think so. Today this ends. You will leave Naureen and never return to her. In the name of the Lord, give me your name."

The jinni looked at her and smiled. "You already know who we are," it said. Rukhsana responded by tightening the ropes around Naureen's feet. When she was certain the ropes were secured, she hoisted her friend up onto the kitchen island.

She sped to the stove, turned off the burners, grabbed all the knives from around the kitchen and shoved them into a drawer. When the immediate dangers were attended to, she cleared the floor around the island, and began.

"In the name of the Most Gracious and Most Merciful, I order you to leave this body. I order you to cease tormenting this soul. Return to the hellfire where you belong."

"This is boring, Rukhsana. Let's do something fun." The jinni grinned at her, pushing out loose teeth with its tongue. Naureen's body stiffened and rose from the counter. The ropes caught alight, causing them to singe her skin and clothing. Rukhsana threw Zamzam at her, but the jinni batted the bottle from her hands. Glass shattered at Rukhsana's feet, doubling her heart rate.

She brushed the shards aside using the sole of her slipper. Naureen's body shifted into a sitting position.

"Look at you," she taunted. "Reduced to a few parlor tricks and outdated methods. You're all the same, fading relics in this new era. No one believes in your God anymore, Rukhsana. Not Naureen, your parents, the world, or even me. Give up and live the life you were meant to have."

"I am living," Rukhsana replied.

"Don't deceive yourself. D'Angelo sees it, and so do you. Your parents messed you up. You should have a husband and children. Instead, you're here in your bathrobe at three in the morning, peering into Naureen's empty eye sockets."

Rukhsana stepped back. "I've chosen my path."

"And how many lives have been lost because of your choice?" Tears streamed down Rukhsana's cheeks as an image of Daniyal and his mother flashed in her mind. Despite the danger, she turned away from the demon.

"Your father advised you to stop, but you're too arrogant, believing you can fix the world. They planted the seed that you're special, but you're not. Rukhsana, you're nothing, and you know it. Otherwise, we wouldn't be back here, would we?"

Rukhsana turned and faced the jinni. "I was put on this earth to protect the innocent from people like you. To exorcise you. I am a raaqi!"

"How sad. If that's all your God gave you as a purpose in life, you should lay down and die right along with your friend."

The corners of Rukhsana's mouth twitched.

"Looks like I struck a nerve," the demon said. The temperature dropped and cold air stiffened Rukhsana's fingers as she rubbed them in the worn down Quran's cover. The familiar monologue of self-doubt surfaced, tying Rukhsana's stomach in knots.

"We came back to watch you squeal and beg for your friend's soul. But the interesting thing is watching as your sole purpose crashes before your eyes. What will you do with yourself now that you've failed at the one thing your parents taught you to do? You failed a t nurse, and now this. You're obviously not good enough to live."

"I've always been good enough," she said. Her eyes looked in the direction of her friend's body, not daring to meet the demon's gaze.

"Really? Is that why your best friend is sitting here with no eyes? Do you know she tried to fight us on her own using science because she believed your mother had brainwashed you? Naureen started believing her own psychobabble and keeping a journal on how to release you from your parents' abuse."

Rukhsana frowned. "That's not true. Naureen is a believer."

"Is she? That's not what it says in there." The demon pointed at a small notebook on the counter next to where the cutting board had been. Cold sweat gathered on Rukhsana's forehead. She walked over to examine it. The black and red notebook lay open, its contents written in Naureen's hand.

Rukhsana turned to the demon who waited with a menacing grin stretching Naureen's red lips to the limit. The empty eye sockets made her expression all the more eerie. Rukhsana wiped the slickness from her hands on her terry cloth robe. Whether she exorcized the demon or not, there was no returning to normality for her friend, and she was to blame.

Flipping through the pages, she caught detailed snippets of analyses constructed through the lens of a practicing psychologist over the duration of the last two years. A secret case study.

"SubhanAllah, Naureen..."

Words like "psychoses," "delusions," and phrases such as "firm belief in mythological beings" and "a danger to vulnerable parishioners" leaped off the page. Rukhsana's fingers trembled as she flipped through the pages, some dog-eared and highlighted, others circled in red ink with a mocking tone, and ayats from the Quran scrawled in the margins. She encountered unfair speculations that left her unable to defend herself or her parents.

"She sounds more like a scientist than a believer. We know that the two can coexist, but at the end of the day, one must choose their path. Your friend chose. She is a kafir, a nonbeliever."

"No." Rukhsana slammed the notebook shut with a definitive slam. "I've seen her pray. She fasts..." Rukhsana readily defended Naureen while her mind struggled to produce proof. When had she last seen Naureen pray? Had she fasted for Ramadan? Was it her responsibility to monitor her adult friend?

"Your friend is a kafir and a liar. She feigned belief in your religion while harboring resentment for all of you. If we were in your position," the demon said, leaning closer, "we would surrender that dirty snake to us!"

CHAPTER TWENTY-ONE

"ALL UNITS, requesting backup. Officer in pursuit of stolen squad car... Well, it's not stolen exactly... goddamn it, where is everybody?" D'Angelo gripped the steering wheel as he chased after Officer West's hijacked corpse in her squad car. The entire scenario felt as though he were on a runaway rollercoaster in a fever dream. He pulled up close enough to read the license plate and stared into the vehicle.

His eyes focused on the rearview mirror, and a horrid realization made the pit of his stomach lurch. There was nothing visible in the mirror but a headful of bouncy brown curls on Rosa's backwards head. The horrid thing, illuminated by his headlights, stared at him. What used to be the gentle face of a smitten woman was now a jeering abomination.

How in the hell could this be happening? He pulled alongside the vehicle. If he emptied his weapon into it, would it die? Before he had the chance to find out, a horn blared, and he found himself bathed in oncoming headlights. D'Angelo veered left onto the empty sidewalk, avoiding a head-on collision by seconds.

Adrenaline surged inside him, sending shockwaves through his extremities until his hands shook on the steering wheel. When the danger passed, he entered the road again in pursuit of the rogue police vehicle. The demon powering Rosa's body had a significant lead on him now.

He pressed the pedal into the floor which had little effect on the speedometer. Damned cruiser. The thing had such a delayed pickup that he lost sight of Rosa's car. For years, the department had sought more powerful vehicles for this very reason.

The one benefit he had was his knowledge of the streets. He knew them like the back of his hand, having grown up in the city. With a little luck, he could take a shortcut and stop the demon before it got away. God help them if it reached Rukhsana's house before he could.

D'Angelo turned off the siren and perked up his ears. There weren't many cars on the road this early in the morning, especially with the amount of fog pouring across the streets. A prickly sensation down his spine made him slow down as the thick condensation enveloped the car. The fog's behavior felt unnatural. He had never experienced such a phenomenon and didn't want any surprises.

He picked up the radio. "Is anybody out there? Michaels? Single-ton... Johnson? Where the hell are you guys?" Static was the only response. Frustration set in his clenched jaw until he thought he'd break a tooth.

His fingers fumbled around the console; he cut the emergency lights. Even with his high beams activated, the fog was as thick as soup. He felt like a sitting duck but had no choice except to continue. What had been sheer determination morphed into a heavy sense of dread. He reached into his pocket and dialed Rukhsana's number, but it went straight to voicemail. He dialed again, getting the same result. "Dammit Rukhsana, answer!"

D'Angelo drove blind in the fog, hoping to God that he didn't slam into anyone, or anything for that matter. From what he could surmise, he was still in the correct lane, though he couldn't see the lines on the road at all. It was risky to drive without his police lights in these condi-tions, but he didn't want to give away his position.

As he progressed, his nerves faltered. His eyes refused to meet the rearview mirror or check his blind spots in the side mirrors. He feared seeing Rosa's face and that hideous grin, or worse, the back of her head. It seemed that he had traveled an especially long time down the road, way longer than needed to get to the turnoff. He eased on the brakes and looked around, though stopping in the middle of the road terrified him. What if the demon were waiting to smash him to bits with the police cruiser?

After the events he had witnessed tonight, nothing appeared implausible. What he might have dismissed previously as hallucinations and stress now felt undeniably real. Evil manifested itself in the worst ways. Despite Rukhsana's repeated attempts to convince him that she and her father were engaged in ongoing battles with malevolent forces, he had always taken her words as metaphorical—until now.

Forced air wafted into the car's interior from the vents. D'Angelo cut the fan off. Cold air persisted, filling the interior. It appeared to have drawn the fog inside, acting like a sentient passenger. He attempted to dispel it by waving his hand, the moisture in the air stubbornly clinging to his skin with each swipe.

"Damn." A rotten stench clung to him, far worse than any corpse he had encountered in his lengthy career. He proceeded to smear it on his bloody hospital gown and the passenger seat. Changing the settings to force the air out did no good. More air forced itself inside. He held his breath and rolled down the window, exacerbating the problem. The stench made him gag. There was no escape from it.

A refreshing gust of wind brought relief as it swept through. The fog gradually dissipated from the road, making it easier for him to orient himself. While the stench in the cabin diminished, allowing him to breathe without gagging, the chill persisted despite his efforts to activate the heater. Proceeding with caution, he gently lifted his foot off the brake and resumed driving.

He made out the overpass that came before the immediate exit leading to Rukhsana's neighborhood and let out a sigh of relief. It wasn't as bad as he'd feared; he would be there soon. When he arrived, he'd help Rukhsana stave off whatever was headed her way. They would do it together, and he'd show her how dependable he was. She needn't worry in her father's absence. She would come to understand that he was every bit as committed to her as the chief had been. He was all she had now. He'd mention the chief's passing later.

It wasn't that he wanted to hide the chief's death, but it didn't help him look like a hero in her eyes because he hadn't stopped the massacre. He didn't want her to think about how he'd made a promise he couldn't deliver.

No, he would tell her in the aftermath after she expressed her gratitude. When the time was right, he would sit her down and explain that the entire event had been out of his control and that he hadn't had the right religious tools to battle the evil entity on his own. That didn't make him a bad guy, did it?

She'd think he was a hero the way he'd gone after Rosa. Sure, he'd lost sight of her cruiser, but the fog was an act of God, wasn't it? You can't fight God.

Either way, now that her parents were gone, he'd step up and fill the void they'd left behind. The first thing he'd do was be the shoulder she needed to cry on, and then he'd try to persuade her to leave this life behind for good. After today, he didn't want to hear another word about exorcisms, demons, or religion.

To take his mind off the present, he turned onto the exit and fantasized about what she must look like without all those baggy clothes and her hijab. Her face was gorgeous, and from what he could tell, she was slim and fit. He wouldn't mind if she offered herself to him in gratitude after he saved her, but he wouldn't beg for her body. Unlike Rosa, who had been so obvious, he had a sense of self-respect and would never appear desperate in front of Rukhsana. She could take her time, but not too long. Once she came to depend on him, he would gently prod her to get the ball rolling with their relationship.

"Oh shit!" D'Angelo was so caught up in his heroic fantasies that he noticed the police barrier at the exit too late. A hard slam on the brakes and a sharp hit to his forehead against the steering wheel snapped him back to a harsh reality.

The late-night squad was already there, waiting. A smile spread across his lips as relief washed over him. His faithful crew had all shown up. The tension in his body eased, and fatigue quickly set in, replacing his earlier anxiety. He hadn't realized just how worn out he was until now, seeing the boys gathered around their cruisers. Sometimes that hothead Michaels gave him grief when he should've been grateful for the extra overtime shifts, but he always came ready to work. D'Angelo quickly put the car in park and stepped out of the vehicle.

"Hot damn, fellas, I've been trying to call you for the last while. Listen, Rosa—well Rosa's vehicle is out here on the street, and I need you to help me find it before she gets to the chief's house." His hand shielded his eyes from the harsh flashing lights on the vehicles. Bodies of varying height stood beyond the cars at the ready. "Michaels, front and center. The rest of you too," he said, snapping his fingers to convey his sense of urgency.

The men remained in place, silhouettes behind the flashing red and blue lights. D'Angelo cleared his throat and tried again. "Fellas, let's come together here in between the vehicles. Move it, on the double." He clapped his hands twice, expecting them to fall into a loose formation around him like a football team on the field during a timeout. "Guys, what the fuck, I'm talking to you. Can't you hear me?"

He stepped between two of the cruisers and stepped up to Michaels's lanky frame. D'Angelo's mouth hung agape at the sight of the missing eyes and torn flesh on the young deputy's face. Michaels tilted his head in a way that suggested he was watching him. He dared glance at the others. They too were mutilated, some of them beyond recognition.

As quickly as he had approached the outspoken police officer, D'Angelo scurried away from him towards the safety of his car. He yanked open the door and dove inside before the terrors surrounding him made him immobile with fear. In unison, the deputies stepped into the flashing lights, illuminating his dread. There was no hiding from it. They were demons, and he was fucked.

The bits of bloody tissue and bone fragments clinging to their uniforms were what he had assumed was the leftovers of a bloodbath. It was useless to hope that they hadn't suffered. D'Angelo's hands shook as he shifted the car out of park and into reverse.

Behind him, a lone cruiser pulled up until it was on his bumper. The lights on the cruisers switched off, and the car's interior light came on, putting the spotlight on D'Angelo's adversary. In the rearview mirror, Rosa's twisted head righted itself, and the grin stretched beyond what he thought possible on a human face into an angry open maw. *But it's not human. Not anymore.*

The possessed men raised their weapons and pointed them at him. His hopes for an easy escape were doused as Rosa's cruiser revved its engine.

Chapter Twenty-Two

"What's your choice, Rukhsana? Do we sacrifice your friend's life and damn her soul, or will you persist in obstructing us and sacrifice your own future as well?"

Panic gripped Rukhsana's throat. Her friend's chances of survival were slim to none. No one could live through an excruciating experience like this while carrying the spiritual weight of all those demons. They were a heavy burden on the soul, and Naureen's had been tired for too long.

What kind of existence awaited her friend now? Everything she had worked tirelessly to achieve had vanished in an instant. Did Naureen possess the mental resilience to recover from this ordeal? Rukhsana remained uncertain. It had taken years for Naureen to feel comfortable enough to interact with other girls at the institution and form friendships.

Progress had been an uphill battle, as Naureen struggled to grasp social cues that never became instinctual. Often, she came across as blunt, even tactless. Much like individuals with autism, she had learned to conceal her social shortcomings. *Masking.* The scars from her current possession ran deeper than mere physical wounds. She was being violated by more than one entity this time. Naureen was swarmed by legions.

Rukhsana glanced at the monstrous entity perched atop the counter, awaiting a verdict she had no authority to render. Deciding the fate of Naureen's soul was beyond her control, or that of the demons. Yet, deep within her heart, a seed of anger and resentment festered. What if she surrendered Naureen's battered body to the horde occupying it? Death would claim Naureen, freeing them both.

Back in the day, when she was still untouched by puberty, Naureen's body rebelled as her personality darkened and became unrecognizable. The blame belonged to neither of them. Rukhsana didn't choose her upbringing, nor did she ask to become Naureen's guardian. Fate threw them together, but Rukhsana had grown weary of the pairing. Why was it still her responsibility to nurture this woman and be her spiritual protector and friend? Didn't she deserve a life of her own?

"Time is running out, Rukhsana. Will you fight us to keep the girl, or shall we claim her?"

Rukhsana's mouth opened and closed, akin to a fish struggling for air. Why the hesitation? Naureen was more than a friend; she was family, Rukhsana's closest connection in the world, especially if her father didn't survive. So why the uncertainty?

Offering herself as a substitute wasn't an option; reality didn't work like the movies. The demons couldn't inhabit her body. Unlike Naureen, Rukhsana had no trouble invoking her faith to ward off evil. Perhaps therein lies the truth. Did she resent Naureen for her weakness? Rukhsana often wondered why she didn't fight harder against the demonic forces. Couldn't she resist? If only she were stronger, the demons would view her as an adversary, not a plaything.

"What happens if you take her?" Rukhsana asked, horrified by her own question. *How could I even ask such a thing?*

The demon leaned in with a sinister smile. "It doesn't hurt. We take her body, and she goes to where lost souls belong."

"Where is that?" Rukhsana recoiled, her hands aching from wringing them.

The demon's lips spread, exposing a mouthful of blackened teeth, most of which had fallen out on the right side. "The same place where we stuffed your whore mother when she finished fucking D'Angelo."

Rukhsana gasped. Sickness threatened to take over. She backed into the wall and groped at the doorknob. When she found it, she threw open the door and ran into the backyard, not stopping to see if the demon gave chase. She heard it laughing as she unlatched the gate and ran to Naureen's house. There had to be a way to defeat them.

RUKHSANA'S HEART beat like a stallion's hooves pounding a racetrack. Finding the key Naureen had hidden took longer than she anticipated. Liars. Demons told the worst lies and used whatever information they could to twist the knife into your back. She told herself that's all it was when they accused her mother and D'Angelo.

There was no way that her mother had committed adultery, especially not with him. Everyone knew how loyal she was to her father. And D'Angelo... the man had been smitten with Rukhsana since the first time he laid eyes on her. No, this was a seed of doubt thrown in for good measure from the horde. A tactic to break her down and play with her head.

Then why were there tears in her eyes? She turned the lock and ran to the kitchen. What should she be looking for? Rukhsana wiped her eyes and glanced at the spotless room. There were no dirty dishes or the inkling of a crumb on the counter. The food in the fridge was fresh and appetizing. The cupboards were full and the trash emptied. You could eat off the floors here.

She took a glass from the cupboard and filled it with water. Her body felt better after downing the second glass, but the tears didn't stop. Casting doubt on her mother made her heart ache. More than once in the past couple of years, she'd caught her parents arguing about something that she didn't quite hear and couldn't piece together later. She'd assumed it was about retiring from performing exorcisms, but maybe it hadn't been. But then, why would D'Angelo pursue her for marriage if he'd had an affair with her mother?

Number one, it's not true, and number two, it doesn't matter, Rukhsana. Get it together. She took a deep breath and exhaled slowly. There had to be something useful here. The house appeared well-preserved, untouched by humans, almost as if it were a designated historical landmark. There was no sign that anyone had lived there in years, other than the stocked fridge.

Rukhsana meticulously searched every room on the main floor, inspecting closet doors, drawers in the china cabinet's base, and the empty entertainment center with its modest-sized television. Everything remained undisturbed. Moving upstairs, she glanced into the hallway bathroom, finding nothing unexpected. The second and third bedrooms were also well-maintained, with empty dressers for guests who never came.

Sadness swept over Rukhsana as snippets of her friend's life played out in her mind. No true family. No significant other. No children. It wasn't that a spouse or children were signifiers of a successful life, but they were indicators that a person might not end up alone.

Rukhsana grunted. The same could be said for her own life. Now that her mother was gone and her father's life hung in the balance, were she and Naureen so different? No. All they had was each other.

"That's incorrect," Rukhsana refuted, dismissing that line of thought. "We have Allah." She ran her hands down her face, interlocking them beneath her chin. A shiver ran through her body as the cold, life-less air seeped from under the main bedroom's door, seeming to grip her ankles and crawl up her legs until it reached her throat.

She coughed involuntarily as it entered her mouth, leaving a thick, slimy residue on her tongue. Quickly, she closed her mouth and hurried back to the hall bathroom, where she promptly spat into the sink, uttering "Bismillah." Despite her efforts to wash it away with hot water from the tap, the brown spittle stubbornly clung to the sink, refusing to dislodge.

Whatever awaited on the opposite side of Naureen's bedroom door, Rukhsana was convinced that the solution lay there as well. She reached into her pocket, tracing the familiar grooves of the pocket-sized Qur'an, and entered the hallway.

Steeling her nerves, she approached the door, acknowledging that this time, there would be no savior coming to the rescue. The responsibility to contain the evil rested solely on her shoulders, and the consequences were grave for them all if she failed.

CHAPTER TWENTY-THREE

ROSA'S CRUISER BACKED UP, then took off down the road and turned left, leaving D'Angelo staring down the barrels of several guns. Sweat dripped into his eyes but he dared not make one false move as the deputies waited. Either way he looked at it, he was proper fucked.

He could throw the still-running car into drive, slam the pedal to the floor, and hope for the best, or he could cut a sharp left, following Rosa's cruiser down a parallel road, praying he'd catch up and stop the relentless demon before it reached Rukhsana's doorstep. He genuinely wanted to save her—their future depended on it. But first, he had to save himself.

"Shit." He looked at his face in the rearview mirror, noticing lines etched in his forehead that hadn't been there before this harrowing week. Or had they? A sudden onslaught of regret crept up on him. He was thirty-four and still single. Maybe he shouldn't have wasted time waiting on the perfect woman. If he had taken Rosa seriously, she might still be alive. They might have had a family. He might not be getting mowed down by the night crew.

"Fuck that. I know what I want." D'Angelo gripped the steering wheel with his left hand while shifting into reverse with his right. He glanced at the crew who stood there waiting to fire at will upon him.

Had they not been afflicted, he might have joked that he'd never seen them so poised and ready.

They looked fierce and powerful, nothing like the small town cops he knew and loved. He'd given them hell over the years, imploring that they look more professional and menacing in the eyes of the public, and now, he'd give anything to have them back. D'Angelo wiped the tickle at the bottom of his chin. He was crying.

He rolled down the window. "This is it, boys," he shouted. "I'm stepping on the gas, and I'm going after Rosa. And make no mistake, I'm sending as many of you to hell as I can!" D'Angelo paused, waiting for the unresponsive men to make a move. The sound of the idling car rattled in his ears. "Shit."

If he had more time or a clear path, he could think. But he didn't and couldn't stall any longer. *This is some last resort shit.* Last resort. He recalled Rukhsana's mother once saying something to him about disbelief. "When it gets down to it, everybody calls on God. Some just wait until it's the last resort," she had said.

He felt like an idiot, but what was there to lose? "God, save me. Not for myself, but for Rukhsana." D'Angelo slammed his foot on the gas pedal and the cruiser shot backwards at breakneck speed. For once, the damned thing picked up and raced down the street like a racehorse. Almost fast enough to dodge the shotgun bucks turning the cruiser into scrap metal. Shards of glass flew across his body, slicing his fingers down to the bone and leaving deep gashes across his face. His foot remained glued to the floor.

As soon as he had driven beyond their reach, he abruptly hit the brakes. "Holy God, I'm not hit." Despite his disbelief in such matters, it appeared to be a genuine miracle. Not one bullet had entered his body. Putting the car into drive, D'Angelo veered onto the nearest left turn. Although he hadn't quite reached the main road, he was fortunate that these neighborhoods followed a grid pattern, eventually leading to Rukhsana's house.

He turned right at the nearest stop sign. Racing towards her street, he reached up to activate the emergency lights and siren, only to find them non-functional. They had been shot out, along with his left tire and, judging by the steam billowing from the hood like a locomotive, likely his radiator too. He prayed there wasn't any gasoline leaking from the tank, as the sparks from the wheel scraping against the road seemed precarious.

Disregarding the stop signs, he glanced hastily left and right, praying for empty streets at this hour. It struck him that the street lights were extinguished, though the clock on the dash remained frozen at three o'clock. It must be way past that now. With each intersection he crossed, blue and red lights flashed, flanking him on either side. Dread gnawed at his core; the crew were tailing him.

"Come on, come on," he said, coaxing the cruiser with his foot. Though he felt his luck had run out, he needed a little more from God. From the looks of it, he needed a lot. They kept after him, street after street, until he feared they would end up in a catastrophic pileup of epic proportions. Still, he'd made it this far, and Rukhsana's house wasn't far. All he had to do was keep his eyes on the road and watch them as they kept pace alongside him like greyhounds chasing a rabbit around a track.

As he was betting on himself to win, a loud crunch from behind caught him off guard. His head lurched forwards, smashing into the steering wheel. He'd been so caught up in watching his peripherals that he'd neglected checking the rear view mirror. D'Angelo glanced in the mirror where Rosa's hideous inhuman grin awaited him.

The cruiser whined and shook as he coaxed it down the road. The car behind him slowed, then sped up and charged, crashing into him. The body of the vehicle shook and groaned. Again, the charging vehicle slammed into him, this time taking away the bumper.

"Goddamn it." D'Angelo feigned left then right, thinking he could outfox the cruiser if he couldn't outrun it. Time after time, the car kept pace, shattering the back end of the vehicle until the muffler dropped down and dragged along the road.

The situation had become dire. He had to find a way to rid himself of the demon locked onto his tail. The cruiser backed off. D'Angelo sighed in relief. His respite didn't last long before a spray of bullets pummeled the back window, scattering glass throughout the car's interior. His headrest protected him, taking the brunt of the abuse, although a fair amount of glass pelted him in the back of his neck. Blood soaked the top half of his hospital gown. Again, bullets rained down on him, taking out his side mirrors, punching out the right side of the windshield. God, how was he still alive? Desperate, he put the car into cruise control, held the steering wheel steady with his hip, and returned fire.

Awkward at best, he managed to take out the remaining glass in the back window before nearly slamming into a parked car on the side of the road. He swerved hard and got himself back into the lane. His plan wasn't working.

D'Angelo adjusted the hospital gown, shaking free glass fragments. His blood made the garment cling to him, and where it wasn't bloody, sweat soaked the cloth. Still, he didn't dare take off his jacket, not with the demon emptying clips of ammo into the car. His jacket didn't possess any magical properties that he was aware of, but he felt a lot more secure wearing it.

Three more intersections. There wasn't much farther to go. The rooftop of the big house across the street from Rukhsana's house was already visible. He had to make it there, get out of the car, and barricade himself inside the house with Rukhsana before the demon ran him down or shot him. The way he saw it, there was no chance in hell of him making it into the house, but he was going to try. It was all for the sake of the woman who would become his wife. Besides, he was her only hope.

The roof of the large house grew bigger, and the flashing lights of Rosa's cruiser activated. As he approached the last intersection, he saw Rukhsana's house. The crew of possessed cruisers had turned and were now poised to reach the intersection. There was a slim chance that he could make it without colliding. He entered the intersection, hoping for the best. Hope wasn't enough. The cruiser smashed in on itself from both sides.

Rosa's car joined the fray, hitting his from the back, packing him into the vessel like a human sardine. The final nail in the coffin came when D'Angelo drove onto the curb and flipped. The car tumbled and rolled down the street, stopped by the lamp post outside Rukhsana's house. He closed his eyes and patted himself all over. Unscathed.

He hung upside-down, locked in by the seat belt, but he was alive.

They were working fast. He heard them clawing at the doors with bloodied hands, the nails long gone from the beds.

D'Angelo gripped his Glock. After some time, they pried the door free. He aimed and emptied his weapon until there was nothing left. Rosa's reanimated corpse stumbled, fell back onto the grass and laughed. A man came out of a house from across the street.

"Aww man, what happened out here?" The man stepped onto the sidewalk and gawked at the cruiser.

"Go back inside!" D'Angelo didn't need a concerned citizen in the way.

"Hey, officer, what happened?"

"Go away." The last thing he wanted was another victim entangled in this mess. "Go home and call nine-one-one. Tell them to send someone from a neighboring department."

The man bent down and clutched his knees. "Are you hurt?"

"Go back inside and do what I said, damn you." D'Angelo released his seat belt and crashed into the roof. The cuts on his scalp bled as fragments of glass dug deeper into his head.

"I'm trying to help you, buddy. I think you're in shock."

It was him who went into shock. Officer Michaels ran him through from balls to sternum with his favorite hunting knife. The man looked down at himself and watched his eviscerated organs steam in the crisp morning air. He fell to his knees, dead before he hit the ground.

In the distance, a piercing scream and a slammed door gave him hope that the cavalry would be called. In the meantime, he had to find a way to get to Rukhsana. Things were looking bleak. He reloaded his Glock, then the thing that had been Rosa pointed her weapon at him. He wasn't sure who shot first.

CHAPTER TWENTY-FOUR

THIRTY MINUTES AGO

A delicate sheet of ice coated Naureen's bedroom door. Rukhsana extended her hand to grasp it, feeling the ice crackle under her touch as she turned the knob. The cold was so intense that Rukhsana had to exert effort to release her fingers. With a gentle push, the door creaked on its hinges, intensifying her anxiety. The erratic nature of demonic possessions kept her on edge, her breath catching as she braced for the sudden eruption of evil from the room.

The odor of fecal matter and decay anchored her in the doorway. Her fingers fidgeted in her sweater pocket, channeling her nervous energy. From her vantage point, she gazed into the room, observing the eerie amber glow cast by the nightlight on the far wall. This illumination contrasted with the shadows created by the bluish hue of the morning sky seeping through the double-wide window. As the rising sun emerged from behind the clouds, the demons played tricks on her eyes. She was back in Naureen's childhood home. The bedroom was still the same after all these years, right down to the busted glass from the storm that left Umm Sayyida's children without a mother. Despite this, she stepped into the room, resolute in her determination to uncover the cause of her friend's possession.

Experience said to check the usual locations first; under the bed, in the nightstands, under pillows. She flipped the switch, surprised that it worked. Rukhsana dropped to her knees and checked under the bed. Except for a storage bin with clothing packed away for warmer days, it was clean. The nightstands were completely empty, as was the dresser. On top, there lay a Qur'an covered in a thick layer of dust, but otherwise, in pristine condition. Otherwise, there wasn't much in the way of clutter.

She tried remembering the last time she had actually been to Naureen's house. It had been some time ago, when she'd blessed it. Rukhsana remembered blessing every room in the house before she allowed her friend to live there. Even so, Naureen didn't spend much time there. Ever the dedicated therapist, Naureen spent the majority of her days and nights at the hospital. When she wasn't there, she was at Rukhsana's house, cooking, chatting, being the sister she never had.

Possession wasn't spontaneous; it didn't happen overnight. It wasn't about an invitation but rather a failure of preventive measures. Her clients were prime examples of this. Despite coming from religious backgrounds and being respected within their communities, many lacked true faith or lived double lives. Some performed rituals of purification and prayer, yet still remained susceptible. In either case, possession was a gradual process, with demons preying on those who left the door ajar.

After all they'd done to bring Naureen back from the brink of her spiritual hijacking, they were back at square one. Rukhsana was tired, and if she was tired, Naureen must be near the end of her rope. The poor woman had no one to depend on but her, and she didn't know if what she had left in the tank was enough.

Rukhsana approached the closet door. "Bismillah." It swung open abruptly. A single breath into the dark walk-in revealed the source of the mysterious foul odor. Widening the door as much as possible, she allowed her eyes to acclimate to the darkness. Spotting the string for the overhead bulb, she pulled it and was taken aback.

Heaps of soiled clothing lay on the floor, alongside a white pillow so heavily stained and greasy at its center that it had darkened, like the blackened peel of an overripe banana. A swarm of flies circled, then settled once more in the corner where Naureen used the toilet, perched over old lab coats and scrubs. She had been occupying the space as her living quarters, if one could call it that.

Instead of Naureen's prized vintage shoe collection, the shelves displayed several black goat heads in various stages of decay, stacked on a makeshift altar with candles and occult symbols. Underneath them, goat legs and other unidentifiable parts littered the floor.

Rukhsana gagged and stepped backwards. The door swung inwards, hitting her in the backside. She landed on dirty clothing, next to a pile of human waste. The lights went out and the door slammed shut.

"Naureen! Please open the door. Let me out." Rukhsana rushed to the door and pounded on it with both fists. "Naureen." She tried twisting the knob. There was no lock, but it wouldn't budge. Using her shoulder, she rammed into the door. Unyielding to the bashing, she found it difficult to overpower the forces holding it closed.

Behind her in the dark space, she felt the air shift. Pausing, she strained to hear amidst the darkness. A deep groan emanated from the area near the shelf adorned with goat heads. Goosebumps covered her flesh. She shuddered.

A spontaneous flame lit one of the half-melted candles on the altar. Rukhsana froze in place. The supplication escaped her lips in the form of a weak whisper, barely passing through her lips. "Bismillah." Somewhere deep in the recesses of the closet, she heard something akin to a beating heart.

Dread worked its way into her nerves until her extremities felt cold. Rukhsana backed into the door, her fingers working overtime, agitating the Qur'an in her pocket. "Bismillah." The beating grew louder. She tilted her head, curious. "Bismillahir Rahmanir Raheem." It emanated from the pile of animal remains.

Approaching with caution, she choked on the foul odors assaulting her senses. Rukhsana coughed, grappling with the overpowering stench. Retrieving a candle from the altar, she consecrated it to dispel any enchantments and shed light on the chaos. Using the toe of her slipper, she prodded the debris, uncovering a pulsating bladder nestled within. Something was stitched within the organ.

Scanning the altar for tools, she spotted a small dagger adorned with a pentacle etched into the handle. Taking hold of it, she began dissecting the thick cords securing the bladder. As she severed the knotted end, she carefully unraveled the rest, releasing a swarm of black flies that obscured her vision. Waving them aside with the flame, she extracted the contents using the dagger.

Among them lay a handful of miniature dolls crafted from sticks and hair, each bearing eerie resemblances to members of the community —police officers donning crudely-sewn uniforms, with one notably attired in a different colored shirt, adorned with a tiny star. "Abi," she murmured. Tiny holes punctured the body, while others were missing eyes, or bore twisted heads with grotesque grins. *Rosa.* Trembling, she set them aside and examined the last object within the bladder—a beating heart.

Branded with three sets of initials—H.H., V.R., and R.D.—she pondered their significance. She was one hundred percent certain that V.R. was Victor, and she was R.D., but who was H.H.? She had a sudden ache for her newly-discovered kin. If he were here, he'd know. It was her fault that he wasn't. She'd been cold the last time they had spoken, and now, she was on her own.

She selected a cloth from one of the dirty piles to gingerly lift the heart, its beat growing more insistent in her grasp. Placing it near the closet door, she began reciting over it. Instantly, the fabric began smoking. Rukhsana turned away too late, having inhaled the acrid smoke emerging from the heart.

Inhaling into her sleeve provided her lungs with respite, restoring clarity to her thoughts. She covered the heart with another piece of fabric then tested the door handle, which finally yielded. Without delay, Rukhsana swiftly collected the bundled heart and dashed out of the closet. The door closed behind her with a resounding slam, a clear indication to refrain from further investigation for the time being. She had uncovered what she sought.

Outside, the tumultuous cacophony of a car crash seized her attention. From what she could tell, the vehicle had somersaulted several times. Her nurse's instincts took over. In no time, she was at the window drawing back the curtains and raising the blinds to survey the scene. Several police cars littered the road, one of them notably more damaged than the others. "Oh no," she muttered, opening the window to get a better look.

The officers in the less damaged vehicles climbed out and surrounded the other one. Rukhsana gasped. Their eyes were missing, like the dolls she'd found in the closet. Like Naureen. They clawed at the car like ravenous predators besieging trapped prey. D'Angelo. They converged upon him, having pried open the door. Rosa approached and D'Angelo shot her. She fell to the pavement and got up again. Never had Rukhsana witnessed this level of evil.

A neighbor came out of his house, and Officer Michaels fell upon him with a weapon. She clutched the heart in her hands and withdrew from the window. Rukhsana barreled down the stairs and out the front door. On her way down, she heard more gunshots.

THE SITUATION HAD REACHED levels beyond any nightmare she'd ever had. Rukhsana opened the door and stepped onto the porch. "D'Angelo!"

"Rukhsana, go back inside. There's too many of them." He rolled out of the vehicle and righted himself.

"You've been shot," she said, spotting the bullet hole in his gut. He pressed against it with his left hand. Another shot rang out and D'Angelo fell to his knees. "No!" Officer Michaels grinned. Rukhsana gripped the bundle in her left hand. "In the name of Allah, the Most Gracious, the Most Merciful, I order you to leave this vessel."

The possessed crew assembled around D'Angelo as he tried dragging himself towards the house. They pointed their weapons, poised to shoot. Rukhsana watched in horror as he bled out onto the street. Besides his audible struggles, an eerie silence blanketed the street. There were no sirens in the distance, no heroes willing to run out and help. They were on their own.

With profound determination, she delved deep into her recitation, invoking the most potent ayats from the Qur'an to expel the spirits from the police officers. Her confidence surged as she observed their weapons trembling in their grasp. Ensnared by the impassioned delivery of divine scripture, they stood there, helpless. Shotguns dropped, and she advanced towards D'Angelo as he approached the curb. The demons recoiled as she set foot on the sidewalk, bolstering her resolve. She had them under her sway, yet she required more.

"That's it, come to me," she said. Their trance broke as her recitation paused, and they resumed aiming their weapons. Rukhsana picked up where she left off. Again, she staved off the attack, locking them into place. When she reached D'Angelo, she knelt and laid the bundle on the sidewalk next to him. He grabbed her feet, using her as leverage as he rolled halfway onto his back. Sadness enveloped her as she saw the dark stains on his abdomen where blood had gathered.

She kept reciting. The demons didn't move, but they were at a clear impasse. Beside her, the heart pumped louder and faster until she was sure it would seize. She recited louder and faster, attempting to outpace the vile thing. Her voice cracked. How much longer could she continue?

Fatigue and stress undermined her efforts, compounded by the urgent need to attend to the dying man. She would have to transport him to the hospital. Suddenly, the front door of her house burst open behind her. Naureen's piercing scream echoed as she descended the porch stairs, brandishing a butcher's knife.

"Naureen, don't!" Rukhsana folded into a defensive posture.

D'Angelo raised his Glock and fired one last shot.

"No! Naureen!" Rukhsana reached out for her friend, but it was too late. The dark smoking hole in the middle of Naureen's forehead oozed black and red. She collapsed in front of them on the sidewalk. Rukhsana rushed to her friend's side and as she knelt, Naureen's body rose from the pavement, levitating.

The knife in her hand caught Rukhsana by surprise. Naureen brought it down into Rukhsana's hand, stabbing her through the palm. Rukhsana screamed in agony and twisted away, taking the embedded knife with her. Naureen's body, still hovering above the ground, twisted until she could wrap her hands around Rukhsana's throat.

Tears ran down Rukhsana's face, as much a reaction to the lack of air in her lungs as to the state of her only friend. It was over. She was too tired to keep fighting. If this was the end, then so be it. She hoped Victor wouldn't take it too hard, if he even cared. And poor Abi. As she began to fade from consciousness, she tried not to think about how he'd react to losing another family member.

A hard tug shifted her body and broke Naureen's chokehold. Rukhsana took in a sharp breath. D'Angelo raised up beside her, shooting Naureen until he'd emptied his weapon. For all his effort, all he'd done was make her into a bloody, pulpy mess. "Rukhsana, the heart, stab the heart!"

She grabbed the knife with her uninjured hand and held it over the beating organ. "Bismillah. May you all return to hell!" Naureen charged. A shotgun barrel dug into Rukhsana's back. As she brought the knife down the world stopped.

Chapter Twenty-Five

THE PRESSURE of the shotgun against Rukhsana's back eased. With caution, she pivoted, seizing the barrel and redirecting it away from her. Michaels loomed above her, frozen in place, his body twitching in response to the disrupted black magic that had controlled him.

Each uniformed body collapsed onto the pavement, forever motionless and lifeless, God willing. She saw the restless evil spirits tear away from each corpse and fade into the morning light. For the first time in hours, Rukhsana felt hopeful; perhaps this marked a turning point in the prolonged horror that had exacted such a heavy toll on her. Naureen lay on the sidewalk, inert and devoid of life, her empty eye sockets offering Rukhsana no discernible expression to hold onto as a final memory. She removed the Qur'an from her bathrobe pocket and draped the robe over her friend.

D'Angelo sputtered next to her. She watched his complexion grow ashen as blood blackened his abdomen. "Let me try to make you more comfortable," she offered, gently cradling his head in her lap. He winced as her hands applied pressure to his most critical wounds. "I'm sorry. This is all my fault. I thought I could get everything under control," she said, tears clouding her vision. "I was too arrogant."

"You were flawless. It's my mistake," he insisted.

"Don't blame yourself," she replied, using her t-shirt sleeve to dab sweat from his forehead.

"If only I had listened to your mother from the start, she'd still be alive. Everyone would," he lamented.

"What do you mean? What does my mother have to do with this?" she inquired, puzzled.

"She tole me your true identity, Rukhsana. I couldn't bring myself to believe the things she said to me about your family, especially the parts about demons and witches. I dismissed it as a joke. I assumed she was losing her sanity. But when the woman in the red dress approached me and requested that I deliver the flowers to Naureen, I complied."

Rukhsana paused. "My true identity... She knew we had extended family. What woman in a red dress? The one who attacked Abi?"

He nodded. "Before all this, she came to me at the station." He coughed for a spell then continued. "I was on my way to the hospital to meet Naureen for a therapy session. I needed clearance after an incident involving a shooting. It seemed harmless, you know?"

"D'Angelo, when was this?"

"Three days before your mother died. I dropped off the bundle of flowers at Naureen's office. They were a strange variety."

"Black tulips?" Rukhsana asked.

"Yeah, how'd you know?" He coughed. "Your mother started behaving erratically soon after. Three days later, the law office collapsed." He turned away and spat blood onto the pavement.

Rukhsana stiffened underneath him. "What did she promise you, D'Angelo?"

"She asked that I do her a favor," he repeated.

"But she promised you something. What was it?"

He wouldn't meet her eyes. "She said all I had to do was deliver the flowers. Ease up, Rukhsana, you're hurting me."

Her eyes burned with fury. "My mother and best friend are dead, D'Angelo. Tell me!"

His lips trembled. "She told me that if I delivered the flowers, nobody would block my path."

"And what was promised to you?" She clenched her teeth, fighting the urge to scream at him.

"You. I'd finally have you. I never imagined Naureen would truly become possessed, or that your parents would die."

Rukhsana recoiled, lowering his head to the pavement. She heard sirens somewhere in the distance. D'Angelo's eyes slowly climbed until they met her livid gaze. "You weren't going to tell me that my father died? How did he pass?" She knew the answer before he uttered a word.

"I shot him—but he was possessed. He killed Rosa, and I had no choice. I didn't want to hurt him. I've been trying to protect him all this time, Rukhsana. You have to believe me. None of this was my intention. The woman, she showed me a vision. It was us getting married and having a family. I had your best interests in mind." Blood spurted from his wounds. The red circle staining the pavement grew around them. "I was a fool."

"Yes," she said, staring off into the distance. "And your selfishness has cost us more than you can repay."

He tried to force himself up on one elbow, but the pain was too great. "If I make it, I'll spend every moment making you happy, Rukhsana. Your parents would have wanted me to look after you."

"Don't speak to me about my parents," she said, wiping tears from her cheeks. "In fact, don't speak to me ever again."

"I know you're upset, but this will come out right in the end. You need time. I've waited this long, I can wait some more." He coughed until he was forced to spit. His teeth had gone red. "Can't you work up a little of your magic to undo these bullet wounds?"

"I don't make magic. I stop it in its tracks," she said. "Bullets are not supernatural."

"But these ones were put here by supernatural beings."

Rukhsana collected herself and stood on the pavement next to him.

"Rukhsana, I know it sounds crazy, but I'm a believer now. Do you hear me? I believe."

"Believe what, D'Angelo?"

"In everything. Angels. Demons."

"God?"

"Of course."

"Then why didn't you trust Him to bring us together instead of using the forbidden to force it?"

"Rukhsana, it seemed like the only way. You weren't responding to my advances. We can get through this together, Rukhsana. I'll be here for you as you heal. I'll take care of you."

Rukhsana's heart grew cold as he spoke. The words that once brought her comfort now meant nothing. With a heavy sigh, she distanced herself, her resolve hardening with each passing moment.

"I trusted you, but I cannot forgive what you've done," she said, her voice cold and distant. Ignoring his pleas, she turned away and started walking back to her house, leaving him to his fate. He was dead before the first ambulance reached their neighborhood.

Epilogue

WHAT WAS it about cemeteries that brought rain? Rukhsana stood at the back of the crowd, watching the crowd pay their respects to Detective D'Angelo Wright. The turnout was decent, almost as large as her father's had been. He had known a lot of cops, most local, some state, and a few from up north.

For whatever reason, no one came forward accusing her father of any crime, nor could anyone explain why Officer West and Detective Wright had emptied their bullets into him.

It was speculated that the night crew had been a part of a sinister death cult, hence the missing eyes on all their dead bodies. No cause of death was determined, and the case was quietly brushed aside after internal affairs officers from the Rosewood Hollow Police Department found no evidence to implicate them.

The demon in Naureen was gone, but Rukhsana couldn't shake the constant sensation of someone peering over her shoulder. Watching. Waiting.

She didn't dare go back to the house for more than a few hours to gather her clothing and mementos. Not mementos. Lies. The temptation to toss everything into the garbage, and forget about the people who raised her was there, but in the end, she couldn't go through with it. The lies had been to shield her and the ruqya, a gift to protect herself when they no longer could. Like now.

Not in the mood to issue condolences, or receive them, Rukhsana edged away from the funeral and hurried back to her vehicle as the rain picked up.

Victor would have the answers she needed; she was certain of it. He had all but vanished over the past few weeks, engrossed in some high-profile murder case. She studied the photo of the smiling children she had found among her parents' belongings.

The only one who stood out besides Victor and his twin, Vincent, was a little girl in a red dress. She stared at the camera, sour-faced and defiant, clearly uninterested in being there. Perhaps when she arrived in Rosewood Hollow, they could clarify who the pale woman in the red dress standing near the trees was. Rukhsana tucked the picture into the visor and shifted the car into drive.

Nakia Cook was born in Atlanta, the other Atlanta, in Cass County, Texas. People think she made it up, but if you squint at the map hard enough, you'll find it. Most of her characters live in Rosewood Hollow, Virginia, which she did make up. It takes a lot to spook her, but when it happens, it's usually a small kid standing in the shadows in the middle of the night.

Sign up for Nakia's newsletter for title and cover reveals and information about new releases once in a while.

www.nakiacook.com

www.ingramcontent.com/pod-product-compliance
Lightning Source LLC
Chambersburg PA
CBHW021155130626

46554CB00005B/1832